Diablo – The Secret of Echo Lake

Gabi Adam

Diablo – The Secret of Echo Lake

Stabenfeldt, Inc.
457 North Main Street
Danbury, CT 06811
www.pony.us

*For all those who have realized that the great
adventure of life is living it day by day.*

Chapter 1

"Ricki! ... Ricki! ... Ricki!" Brigitte Sulai called out to her thirteen-year-old daughter as she charged up the stairs to the girl's room from the kitchen. "This is just intolerable ..."

But Ricki couldn't hear the exasperation in her mother's voice over the sound of her own voice singing along off-tune to the latest hit blaring out of the speakers on her CD player. Her feet danced to the rhythm, causing the kitchen light fixture that hung from the ceiling below Ricki's room to swing dangerously back and forth.

Brigitte flung open her daughter's bedroom door. "RIC-KI!!" she yelled into the room, and finally the girl turned around, looking astonished.

"Mom! Is something wrong? Just a minute, I can barely hear you!" Ricki reached over and turned the volume down on the CD player.

Brigitte sighed with relief. "Tell me, are you deaf, or just inconsiderate? We don't live at a carnival! You *are* aware that other people besides you live in this house. Please be a little more considerate of our ears! This constant booming is unbearable!" she scolded.

Ricki was flabbergasted. "Booming! The song is number one on the –"

"RICKI! I don't care if this awful screeching is number one or number one hundred! The volume at which you play it is totally unacceptable! And I've spoken to you about this before."

"Yeah, Mom, I know." Ricki rolled her eyes and breathed loudly through her nose. She was annoyed that the song – one of her favorites – had been interrupted by her mother's reprimand.

"One of these days you're going to make the kitchen light come down with all that stomping! ... Weren't you going to do your homework? How can you concentrate with that music blaring? The new semester only just began and already you're not making an effort to –"

"Please, Mom. I'll get to it right now!" Ricki cut off Brigitte's angry torrent. *It's the same old thing, every day*, she thought, and was relieved when her mother finally turned and left the room.

"The music stays off until you're finished with your homework!" Brigitte called over her shoulder as she slammed the door shut.

"Boy, she's in a great mood today," Ricki said quietly to herself, and reluctantly went over to her CD player and pressed the Stop button.

Lost in her thoughts, she let her eyes swing from her history workbook to the small, framed photo that was standing on her desk in front of her. It was a photo of her black horse, Diablo, as he ran across their paddock.

"You're lucky," intoned Ricki and smiled at the photo. "No one scolds you if you whinny too loudly or stamp the ground with your hooves!" She thought that over for a moment. "Maybe it's because you don't sing out of key! Yeah, that's probably the reason!"

Grinning, Ricki went back to her homework. Thank heavens it was almost finished.

"I don't know how I'll be able to write an essay on Joan of Arc without that music – it helps me think," she mumbled, and then she resigned herself to her fate. One glance at the clock on the wall told her that she had to hurry if she wanted to go riding with her friends that afternoon, and the time they had decided to meet was fast approaching.

*

"Where have you been?" Lillian Bates asked her girlfriend accusingly. "We could have been on our way half an hour ago!"

"That's right!" agreed Ricki's boyfriend, Kevin Thomas, and as if that wasn't enough, Cathy Sutherland joined in as well.

"What's up, Ricki? You have the shortest distance to get here. All you have to do is walk out of your house and into the stable. We have to ride our bikes to get to our horses!" Ricki just looked away and hurried over to Diablo's stall. Quickly, she began to groom him.

"Joan of Arc messed me up," the girl began her defense. "That stupid extra essay in history almost made me crazy!"

Kevin and Cathy grinned openly. They were in the same class as Ricki. How could they forget what their teacher said as he gave Ricki the extra essay to write as a punishment?

"If Miss Sulai thinks she is still on vacation and can disturb my class with her irrelevant comments, then she's mistaken. Ricki, you haven't been paying attention for the last few classes. There's more to life than just those scribbles you make during the lessons when you should be listening! What's *that* supposed to be? A cow? Or maybe it's a camel?" With a smirk on his face, Mr. Raymond had pulled out Ricki's artwork from under her pad and showed it to the entire class.

"It isn't *supposed* to be anything. That is my horse, Diablo. And I have been listening!" Ricki stammered defensively with a bright-red face.

The teacher nodded. "Oh! So, it's a horse! Well, actually, it's completely recognizable, at least with a little imagination. A horse's hoof is clearly –"

Before Ricki could say another word, Mr. Raymond's voice had boomed over the laughter of the entire class.

"Since I don't give grades in art, just in history, I won't voice my opinion further on the subject of these scribbles! But in order for me to see if you've been following my class, I want you to write an essay on Joan of Arc for the next session. I'm sure that won't be a problem for you. All you really have to do is repeat what I said."

"Oh, no, Mr. Raymond," exploded Ricki. "That's not fair! It's such a beautiful day, and I don't want to spend my time with some old story out of the past."

"You can illustrate your essay with mysterious sketches," her teacher added calmly. "And I expect you to write at least three pages!"

"What? *Three* pages? That can't be –"

"Make that four pages!"

"Why?" Ricki was beginning to get angry. This old slave driver was the worst!

"Every time you ask 'why' the length will increase by one page!"

Ricki had just taken a breath to say some thing else, but after Mr. Raymond's threat she decided it would be smarter to keep her mouth shut. After all, she didn't want to spend the whole afternoon in her room.

*

"Extra homework? That's not so bad. But writing an essay as a punishment? That's not so good!" Kevin leaned casually against the side of the stall, behind which his roan, Sharazan, was impatiently scraping away the straw with his hooves.

"Oh, be quiet!" Ricki threw her currycomb over the sliding door and pulled her hoof pick out of her back pocket.

Diablo looked at her apprehensively. He sensed that Ricki wasn't in her usual good mood.

"Raymond is an arrogant donkey ..." Ricki grumbled to herself, but Lillian stopped her before she could continue.

"Be careful what you say! Chico would never forgive you if you compared your teacher to him!" she laughed and glanced over at her donkey, who was sharing one of the larger stalls with Salina, the newly adopted pony mare.

"That's true! That would really be an insult!" nodded Ricki.

"For whom? For Raymond, or for the donkey?" asked Cathy, who was just then pulling the snaffle over Rashid's head, the horse she took care of.

9

"For Chico, of course! What a question!" Ricki laughed. "Come on, let's hurry! I have the feeling that a gallop across the fields is the only thing that can drive Raymond and Joan of Arc out of my head!"

"Well, we have no problem with that," replied Lillian as she led her snow-white Doc Holliday, saddled, out of the stable.

Ricki began to sweat as she saddled Diablo with lightning speed.

"Man, am I stressed out!" she groaned, and wiped the sweat off her forehead with her red bandana.

"Ricki ... Ricki! ..." Brigitte Sulai's voice boomed across the yard.

"What now?" Ricki wondered aloud. The girl led her black horse out of the stable and pressed the reins into Lillian's hand. "I'll be right back," she said and ran off with an agonized look on her face.

"I'm beginning to wonder if we'll ever get going today," Cathy said as she leaned against the muscular neck of her dun horse and rubbed him gently between the ears.

"What's up?" Ricki called to her mother from what she thought was a safe distance.

"Would you mind coming over here to me, please?" Brigitte asked. Ricki got a bad feeling when she saw the frown on her mother's face.

"Didn't you promise me that you were going to clean your room today? It's looked like a pigsty now for weeks."

"I'll do it tonight!" Ricki tried to calm her mother down.

"I've heard that before."

"I promise I'll do it! Cross my heart! As soon as I get home!" Ricki put all of her persuasive charm into these last words.

10

"Oh, all right!" her mother replied. "But if you renege on your promise again, you'll be forbidden to go to the stable for a week!"

Ricki burst out laughing.

"Mom! You're going to forbid me to enter my own stable? You're not serious, are you?"

"Oh yes, I am! Don't you doubt it for a second!" Brigitte's eyes flashed with anger.

Is everyone around me going crazy? Ricki asked herself, not daring to say it out loud. She turned around slowly, hoping that her mother wouldn't call her back again.

As soon as she was back with her friends, she grabbed Diablo's reins and, with a desperate look at her friends, said, "Let's go, people, let's get out of here! My mother is in the same kind of mood as Mr. Raymond. You'd think they were related."

"Where are we going to ride to?" Kevin asked as he mounted his horse.

"Doesn't matter!" responded Ricki. "Wherever! The main thing is for me to get out of my mother's field of vision!"

*

As soon as the Sulai farm disappeared from view, Ricki felt herself start to relax.

"Is there a full moon tonight or something?" she asked as she bent over and gave Diablo a huge hug around his neck.

"Why? Does your mother transform herself into a werewolf? Do you have to chain her up in the cellar?" joked Cathy.

"Don't be silly. But haven't you guys ever noticed how a

11

lot of people get very aggressive – and weird – whenever there's a full moon?"

"If that's the case, then as far as Mr. Raymond is concerned, there would have to be a permanent full moon," laughed Kevin. He shortened Sharazan's reins.

"What was that about a gallop and filling our lungs with fresh air?" he asked and got an immediate and enthusiastic, "Yeah!" as a response from all three girls. And the young quartet of horse lovers gave their horses free rein and galloped over the harvested field.

I love this so much, thought Ricki, as the motion of her body adjusted itself to the rhythm of her horse's gait. Diablo seemed to glide rather than gallop. His rider could hardly feel it when his hooves touched the soft ground.

May the path of happiness be eternal, the happiness that comes to the rider of the flying horse, at the moment of recognition.

Where did I read that? Ricki asked herself. She had suddenly remembered the verse but it seemed too beautiful a day to worry about who had written it. She bent lower and lower over Diablo's neck and seemed to sink completely into his long, flowing mane.

He is wonderful! thought Ricki happily, gazing lovingly at the ears of her beloved horse as they dipped up and down. She realized once again that there was nothing in the world that she would trade for her black horse.

"Look out! There's a ditch up here!" yelled Kevin, who had been riding in front. His warning jolted Ricki from her reverie.

Ricki quickly reined in Diablo and brought him to a

12

standstill in a few more steps. Had she not, he would have leaped over the ditch.

"Oh, wow! Thanks, Kevin!" the girl shouted, out of breath. She wasn't sure that she would have made the jump without trouble. She was a good rider, but she knew she had a problem with some jumps.

"Hey, what do you guys think about visiting Carlotta?" Lillian turned around in her saddle and looked at her friends. "Let's see how the construction on her retirement farm for aging animals is coming along!"

"Great idea!" said Cathy and patted Rashid's neck. "This good boy hardly ever gets to see his owner anymore."

It was true. In the last few weeks Carlotta Mancini had been in the Sulais' stable only a few times to visit her former circus partners Rashid and Sharazan. But since selling Sharazan to Kevin and turning over the care of Rashid to Cathy, she knew that they were in good hands, and so she didn't worry about them. On the other hand, she spent a lot of time fighting with various workers who were supposed to be hurrying with the changes being made to the beautiful old farm she had inherited. Two additional bathrooms were being built in the farmhouse and several dividing walls were to be constructed on the second floor in order to create a few small rooms. Carlotta was planning to accommodate some of her friends on the farm as guests.

The former dark cowshed, where Salina's owner had kept her before he died, was going to be converted into a large horse stable. That meant that spacious stalls, large windows, and saddle and feed rooms had to be built. To keep everything under her control, Carlotta was even thinking of moving into the little apartment on the ground floor of the farmhouse, although she owned a large house a few miles away, where she lived, together with Kevin and his mother, who did all the housework for her.

"Let's just wait and see what happens," Carlotta said whenever the kids asked her about her plans.

Lillian's suggestion to visit the older woman went over well not just with Cathy, but with Kevin and Ricki too. They nodded in enthusiastic agreement and guided their horses in the appropriate direction.

"Maybe we can help with something," the boy said, flexing his muscles.

"If you have any extra energy, you can offer to help Jake this evening. He'd be really pleased if you took over cleaning out the stable for him," Ricki joked. She leaned over and pinched her boyfriend in his biceps.

"I was going to do that anyway," Kevin claimed and let his thoughts wander to the old stable hand. Jake Alcott, from whom Ricki had received Diablo as a present some time ago, and who now took care of the horses in the Sulais' stable, wasn't as young or as healthy as he once was, and the four friends couldn't help but see that it was becoming hard for him to maneuver a heavy wheelbarrow full of manure or carry bales of hay or straw through the stable.

"I'd do more in the stable to help, too, but Jake, that stubborn old mule, always wants to do everything himself!" responded Ricki, more to herself than to the others, and she shook her head in exasperation. She loved the old man like a grandfather and had learned so much about horses from him. "Sometimes I'm afraid that he'll just collapse! He's already had one heart attack, but he doesn't want to think about it!"

14

"I have the feeling that he just wants to prove to himself and to us that he's not ready to retire yet. Don't you think so?" Cathy blinked in the sunshine and then sneezed just as she finished talking.

"Bless you!" the others shouted in unison, and then they began to count.

"Let's see if you get into the *Guinness Book of Records* today," commented Lillian and observed her friend closely.

It really was a phenomenon. Every time Cathy looked up at the sun she had an attack of sneezing that usually lasted for at least fifteen lusty sneezes. Today was no exception.

"Seventeen ... eighteen ... nineteen ..." counted Ricki, and Cathy could hardly get her breath.

"Wow! Twenty-two times! Cathy, you broke your own record!" grinned Kevin, as the girl sat in her saddle exhausted.

"Look," Lillian said, pointing ahead to Carlotta's farm, which had come into view. "It looks like all the carpenters in town are working out here today. I'm guessing we'll just be in the way!"

"Do you think we should go someplace else?" asked Cathy and looked at her friends undecidedly.

"Course not! At least we can drop in and say hello, even if we stay for just a minute. Anyway, she's always glad to see us," Ricki said. The four of them continued riding toward the farm and arrived about twenty minutes later at Mercy Ranch, as the farm was unofficially called.

Cars were parked everywhere. The heating technician, electrician, mason, plumber, and several carpenters had been working since early morning.

The kids guided their animals carefully between the cars

15

in order to get to the open front door, through which loud hammering and drilling could be heard.

"Car-lot-taaa, are you here?" Kevin had pressed Sharazan's reins into Ricki's hand, ran up the three front steps to the door, and was now peering into the house.

"Car-lot-taaa ... " he called again, and a moment later the older woman came out of the stable door and smiled at the youngsters merrily.

"How nice that you've come to visit me!" She ran her dusty hands over her sweaty face and left dark gray smudges behind.

"Hey, Carlotta, you look like you've turned into a clown! You've decorated your face with grease paint," teased Ricki and received a light knock on the head as response.

"Don't be so fresh, young lady!" laughed Carlotta and hobbled over to Rashid, leaning on the crutch that she'd needed ever since her circus accident. "My sweetheart! How nice to see you! I see you're doing well! Just wait, soon I'll have more time for you!"

"Are you making good progress with the renovations?" Lillian wanted to know, and Carlotta nodded energetically.

"Yes, I can't complain. The inside walls are already finished, the carpenter is putting in the doors for the rooms, and the masons are busy in the stalls." Carlotta's eyes glowed. "Let me tell you ... if all of this ends up looking like I imagine it in my dreams, the future tenants of this stable will feel as though they are in paradise!"

"I can imagine," nodded Ricki. She knew that Carlotta wouldn't do anything halfheartedly. When this determined old woman decided to do something, she didn't rest until everything was done just the way she wanted.

16

"How are Jonah and Salina?" Carlotta asked as she stroked Rashid lovingly along his neck.

"Salina said that she misses her daily ration of carrots, and Jonah has managed to get my father to do anything he wants. I think if he stays in our stable much longer, Dad won't let him go," Lillian answered. She had to laugh when she thought about the gigantic old draft horse that Carlotta had saved from being sent to the slaughterhouse, and who was temporarily housed at the Bates farm. The old horse had simply won over Lillian's father Dave with his enthusiastic affection. The clever animal had observed how the catch was opened on the door to his stall, and now Jonah kept escaping and going on a tour around the farm for himself. As soon as he saw Dave Bates he went over to him and followed him around like a dog. There seemed to be a special connection between the two of them.

Carlotta grinned and was about to say something when a carpenter leaned out of a window and called to her.

"Boss, can you come over here a minute? I think they gave me the wrong door!"

Carlotta waved up to him so that he knew she had heard him and prepared to go.

"As you can see, I don't even have time for a little talk, but in a few days it will be different! Maybe I'll drop by this evening." She hobbled into the house as quickly as she was able.

"Whoa, I think we really are in the way," realized Ricki and swung herself back up into the saddle. "Come on, let's go! Let's ride over to Echo Lake. We haven't been there in a long time!"

"OK!"

17

Happily, the teenagers left Mercy Ranch behind them and started off in the direction of the lake, which was in the middle the woods and incredibly beautiful.

The four friends loved to ride around in the area. Even though a lot of people hiked around it, the lake seemed like a little piece of untouched nature. Ducks and swans brooded in small, almost invisible, coves, covered by the hanging branches of countless weeping willows. The calls of owls and herons echoed over the lake. All in all, this little piece of land transmitted a feeling of tranquility, harmony, and peace. Ricki was always a little sad when she had to leave it to ride back home.

*

As soon as they turned into the woods toward the lake, Ricki had a strange feeling of uneasiness that was completely foreign to her in these surroundings. As she reached Echo Lake, she looked about her, confused and searching for something to explain her feelings, but at first glance everything seemed to be as it always was when she rode here.

Lillian, Cathy, and Kevin talked happily amongst themselves, but when Lillian's laugh echoed through the woods Ricki jerked suddenly, and then she knew what was wrong.

"Hey, be quiet!" she called to her friends, but they just giggled.

"What's the matter, Ricki? Is talking forbidden here all of a sudden?"

"Idiot! Seriously, don't you notice anything?" Ricki had halted Diablo and was listening intently.

"Notice what?" Cathy made a funny face. "Are the greens greener than usual? Or did one of our paths disappear?"

Ricki's eyes flashed. If there was anything she hated, it was moments like this, when she asked something in earnest and her friends didn't take her seriously.

"Could you maybe – just once – spare me your silly comments!" the girl snapped, a little more angrily than she had actually intended.

Cathy ducked her head, insulted.

"Something's wrong! Can't you guys sense it?"

"Ricki, don't be so mysterious! Just tell us what you mean!" responded Kevin, and Lillian nodded in agreement.

"Maybe we're stupid, but I have no idea what you're talking about."

"All right!" Ricki pointed to the tops of the trees. "Usually when we ride through the woods, the birds are chirping nonstop. Sometimes we see rabbits, or even deer. But today there're no quacking ducks, no swans to be seen. It's so quiet ... as though some thick fog has covered the woods and the lake, frightening the animals. Good grief, don't you guys notice it?"

Finally her friends stopped their chatter and listened intently to the silence.

"You're right! There's not a sound. It's not possible that all of the birds are sleeping at the same time, is it?"

"Maybe someone's having a party and they were all invited."

"You know what?" asked Ricki, furious, "I don't need this!" With that, she shortened Diablo's reins and let him walk.

"Wait, we're coming with you," called Kevin, but Ricki acted as if she didn't hear him.

Do what you want, she thought, and decided to find out for herself what was going on here. Let the others think what they want.

"Man, oh man, she's really in a bad mood today!" grumbled Cathy and stuck her tongue out at Ricki, who was riding in front of her.

"I don't know," Kevin warned, looking speculatively at his girlfriend. "When Ricki says that something's wrong, it usually turns out to be true. Maybe we should look around instead of making fun of her!"

Lillian and Cathy looked at each other and decided, silently, that Kevin was right.

"OK. Then let's uncover the mystery of the silent woods and the secret of Echo Lake!" grinned Lillian and urged her Holli onward in order to catch up with Ricki.

"Hey, Ricki, don't be mad!" she called breezily, and made a pleading, funny face. "We're just all a little stupid, but at least we have you to set us straight."

Actually, Ricki wanted to stay mad a little longer, but looking at the faces that Lillian was making made her laugh.

"You guys are really idiots, you know that?"

"Of course!"

"Then that's OK with me!"

In the meantime, Kevin and Cathy had caught up with them.

"We –"

"Whoa, Diablo ... easy!" Ricki interrupted her friend, and tried to calm her horse.

20

Diablo had suddenly begun to dance around, and his ears played back and forth nervously. He stretched his head up high and flared his nostrils.

"What's wrong, boy? Did something scare you?" Ricki shortened the reins some more as she felt her horse tense up under the saddle.

"Don't do anything weird, boy," she begged the horse and was shocked when Diablo whinnied loudly.

The other horses started getting nervous, too.

Holli turned around on his hind legs as though there were a danger right in front of him, and Lillian, who hadn't reckoned with his jerky movements, was having trouble staying in the saddle.

"Hey, what's going on? Are you crazy?" she shouted. Her voice frightened Rashid, who jumped to the side and rammed into Sharazan.

Within this chain reaction, Kevin's horse moved backward and slid with his hind leg into a small, shallow ditch that ran along the path.

Quickly Kevin leaned forward and grabbed his horse's neck to keep from sliding out of the saddle. After a moment of fear, with a tremendous jump, Sharazan got out of his predicament and landed back on the path. After a few seconds, Kevin managed to get him under control.

Diablo, who was calm again, just stood there as though nothing had happened.

The four friends, pale as ghosts, just looked at each other. "What was that?" Ricki asked, her voice shaky, but no one knew what to answer.

"I have no idea," responded Lillian, who was a little shook up herself.

The four friends looked around cautiously, but they couldn't find anything that could have caused their horses to spook.

"Should we keep riding or go back home?" asked Cathy, and although Ricki was apprehensive, she said with determination, "Let's keep going! I have to find out what's going on here!"

Chapter 2

Quiet and preoccupied, but extremely wary, the friends rode along the shore of Echo Lake looking for something to explain why the horses had acted so strangely. Nothing seemed to be out of the ordinary, but Ricki found it odd that they didn't see any animals, didn't hear any bird sounds, and didn't encounter a soul out for a stroll on this lovely day in this lovely place. *Very strange*, she thought.

"I just don't get it," Ricki said, as she and her friends guided their horses toward home. "I feel as though I'm in a horror film, and that something awful – some dark spirit – has settled over the lake, the woods, and the animals."

"The fog of terror has struck again," intoned Kevin, with mock gravity. But Ricki's reproachful, get-serious look put an end to his feeble attempt at humor.

"Oh, come on," he said, trying to be helpful. "Let's ride back here tomorrow. The world will look different to us then, I promise. Who knows what's wrong today? ... Remember, Raymond and your mother are not in great moods today either, and if people can be nuts sometimes, then I guess we should let nature have its moods too.

You'll see, tomorrow the quacking of ducks will greet us as we arrive."

Dubious, Ricki gave her boyfriend a sideways glance. "Hopefully," she mumbled, and then she was silent until they got home.

*

The kids had just removed their saddles and were thinking about how to spend the rest of the afternoon, when Jake, accompanied by Lupo, his mangy stable cat, came into the stalls.

Kevin immediately remembered that he had wanted to help the old man with his chores and said, "Jake, how do you feel about taking the evening off?"

"Huh?" The old man looked at him bewildered.

"Free evening! Watch television and stuff –"

"Television? Nothing good on anyway! And the news, all they talk about is the unrest everywhere in the world. I just can't listen to it anymore. Anyway, moving around is the best prevention for the stiffness in my joints, which is start-ing already because I've been standing around jabbering with you too much," commented Jake as he shuffled along the corridor to get a pitchfork.

"Well? What did I tell you? You can't slow that man down!" whispered Cathy. Kevin, however, shook his head and ran off after the elderly stable hand.

"OK! You need to move around? Then go for a walk," he said and smiled at Jake.

The stable hand stopped, pressed his hands into his sides, and stared at the boy sternly.

24

"Say, could it be that for some reason you want to get rid of me? Don't I take good enough care of your horses anymore? Is there anything you want to complain about? Come on, tell me right now!"

Kevin rolled his eyes and groaned loudly.

"For heavens sake, Jake, what do you take me for? We all know that we couldn't wish for a better stable hand. I just wanted to get you some time off. After all, you work here every day, and it wouldn't hurt us to help you with your work sometimes."

"Humph!" grumbled Jake. He pushed Kevin aside and reached for the pitchfork. Grinning, he looked over at Ricki.

"Don't worry about me. If it gets to the point where I can't handle the workload around here any longer, I'll tell you. But you, young lady, you'd better clean up your room. Your mother was here twice already looking for you."

"Oh, darn! I completely forgot about it!" Ricki said, suddenly depressed. "People, I think that's it for me today. By the time I get done cleaning my room, it'll be too late for anything else."

"What if we help you?" asked Lillian enthusiastically.

"No, no, don't worry about it. I don't really need the movement for my bones like Jake, but if my mom finds out that I haven't cleared up the mess myself, I'll be toast."

"OK, then we won't. What are the rest of us unemployed going to do now? We are wanted neither in the stable, nor in Ricki's room, nor at Carlotta's." Lillian looked around the room questioningly.

"Now that I think about it," Cathy interrupted, "my room isn't too neat either. Maybe you –"

"Hang on a minute, Cathy! Has your mother threatened you with anything about it yet?" Kevin tried to derail her train of thought.

"No, but that doesn't mean she won't," she responded.

"Tough, Cathy! We're willing to undertake these cleaning measures only in total emergencies! Let's go swimming instead."

"Great idea!"

"Genius!"

"Terrific!" Ricki joined in the general euphoria and sighed resignedly. "While I'm swimming in dust, you'll be refreshing yourselves in cool water! OK, I guess there's nothing I can do. See you guys tomorrow."

"Yeah, see you!"

"Bye, Ricki. Bye, Jake!"

Kevin gave his girlfriend a quick kiss on the cheek. "I'll be thinking of you," he said softly.

"Later," responded the girl, and she waved to him for a long time, as he and Lillian and Cathy slowly disappeared on their bikes. Ricki walked over to the house, kicking up gravel from the courtyard.

*

Kevin and the two girls had ridden to their respective houses to change into their bathing suits.

"Should we go to the swimming pool or the lake?" asked Lillian, as Kevin finally clamped his bath towel on the back of his bike.

"Swimming pool!" shouted Cathy, while Kevin simultaneously shouted, "The lake, of course!"

"What now?" laughed Lillian.

"Where do you want to go?"

"Well, I'd prefer Echo Lake, too."

"In that case, I guess I'll have to bow to the majority," responded Cathy, trying to ignore the fact that she'd heard that some swimmers had left the lake with leeches on their legs.

Due to an unavoidable delay, brought on by the enormous portions of ice cream that had to be eaten on the way to Echo Lake, the three friends arrived at their destination a little later than they had planned. They didn't see the inconspicuously dressed man on the other side of the lake who was frantically pulling an old rowboat out of the water and hiding it carefully under branches on the ground.

"It's still so quiet here," said Kevin.

"Not for long!" shouted Lillian loudly as she ran to the water. She jumped into the cold water with a scream and then started splashing her friends.

Two minutes later, they were laughing and shouting, playfully involved in a raucous water fight, while the unknown man quietly slipped away.

*

Ricki had piled up all of her clothes on the floor and was just about to tidy up her closet.

"Half of this stuff doesn't fit me anymore," she said to herself, and wondered whether she should get a big plastic bag and put her outgrown things in it to donate to Goodwill. However, before she could decide, she noticed that the sky had suddenly gotten dark, and a low rumble in the distance warned that a storm was brewing.

I hope the others get home before the storm breaks, she thought as she glanced worriedly out of her open window and saw the first bright flashes of lightning.

She was just about to shut her window when she heard the nervous whinnies of the horses in their stalls.

This weather's scaring them, too, she thought, deciding to go to the stable for a few minutes to calm the animals. But just as she was about to leave the room, her glance was drawn to the ceiling light, which had begun to swing ominously.

"What's that?" Ricki asked herself tonelessly and stared wild-eyed at her collection of decorative bottles on the wooden shelf over her bed. They had begun to vibrate.

"Mom ... Mooomm!" screamed Ricki and ran downstairs so fast she almost knocked over her little brother, Harry.

"My ... my house of cards ... it collapsed!" he sobbed with eyes as wide with fright as Ricki's.

Brigitte Sulai came running out of the kitchen, pale as a ghost, and took Harry in her arms.

"Somewhere in the mountains there must have been an earthquake, and we're feeling the aftershock here," she said quietly.

Ricki ran outside shouting, "Diablo! Dear God, please, make it stop! Please, please, please ... I'm so afraid."

Ricki's heart was beating wildly, and she entered the stable completely out of breath.

Bewildered, she looked at Jake, who was sitting calmly on a bale of hay eating his dinner with all of the animals watching.

"Want a piece of ham and cheese?" he asked, completely unruffled, causing Ricki to just stare at him and shake her head in exasperation.

"How can you eat at a time like this? There's ... somewhere there's an earthquake! The ceiling lamp in my room is shaking, and ... and you ... you're just sitting here without a care in the world!" Ricki was floored.

The old man grinned and pointed to a bale of hay.

"Sit down and be quiet! It's just a tremor. Besides, it's over already. It only lasted for a few seconds."

Ricki didn't dare sit down. She was still too frightened. With trembling legs she stumbled over to her horse and stroked him tenderly across his muzzle.

"Are you sure that it's over?" she asked Jake, her voice still a little shaky.

"Yeah," he said. "Do you want something to eat or not?"

Ricki shook her head. Even if she had been really hungry, it would have been impossible for her to swallow even one bite.

She cuddled with Diablo, who enjoyed it as much as she did, while she gazed at the stable hand reflectively.

"It's happened a few times already," he said without sounding upset. "It doesn't happen often, but every once in a while there'll be a tremor. You don't need to be afraid, Ricki. We don't live in a major fault area!"

"Well, I hope the earthquake knows that!" commented Ricki, who heaved a sigh of relief.

"While we human beings aren't aware of what's happening, animals can sense these things way in advance," continued Jake. Suddenly Ricki realized why it had been so still in the woods, and why the horses had behaved so

29

strangely and uncontrollably. Then she told Jake what had happened at the lake earlier in the day.

"See! Now you've learned something new," exclaimed the old man, smiling at her. "By the way, how are you coming with your room?" Jake asked, switching the subject, and Ricki rolled her eyes in response.

"It looks like the aftermath of an earthquake," she laughed with relief. She gave Diablo a big kiss on his soft muzzle and then ran back to the house. She knew she had to finish the job today, because she had promised her mother she would. Otherwise, for the next few days, Lillian, Cathy, and Kevin would have to go riding without her.

They're probably as frightened as I was, she thought as she put her clothes back into the closet. She had completely forgotten that she had wanted to sort out the ones that didn't fit anymore.

*

The next day there were only two topics of conversation in school and among her friends. The first was the tremor, which had horrified them all for a few seconds, and the second was the burglary in the school, which had occurred last night.

Ricki snuggled up next to Kevin's arm as the friends sat together in the stable after school later that afternoon.

"I was really worried about you guys when the storm started up yesterday," she admitted.

"Well, we were a little scared ourselves. The sky blackened so suddenly that we decided to ride back home as fast as we could."

"We just made it in time, I'd say," Lillian added.

"Hey, what do you think about the burglary at school?" Cathy brought up the other big subject as she opened the sliding door to Rashid's stall to lead her beloved horse out onto the corridor. She wanted to groom him.

"What's there to say?" asked Kevin in response. "Probably some idiot wanted to give himself a raise in his allowance."

"Do you think it was a student?" asked Ricki, shocked.

"I have no idea, but since there were no broken windows, and only the locks on the front door and the office door were forced, I'd say that it was someone who knew exactly where the petty-cash box was kept. Since teachers, I think, earn enough, I'd say it must have been a student," replied Kevin, with the self-satisfied manner of a detective.

"Hmm, that sounds convincing."

"Wasn't there a similar case at Valley Middle School about two or three months ago?" Lillian frowned.

"I don't know, but there have been a lot of burglaries in town recently – at Mrs. Lorne's fabric store, Morton's Grocery, and also several private homes. Mom found out about it when she went shopping, and it was also in the newspaper," Ricki explained.

"That's almost like a mystery story," said Cathy as she greased Rashid's hooves.

"I'm so glad I live in the country," interrupted Lillian. "There's nothing to steal at our house!"

Cathy stood up and stretched her tense back, then leaned against Rashid's neck for a moment. "Say, aren't you guys going to groom your horses today? I thought we were going to go riding."

31

"We thought we'd give you a head start. You always need half an hour longer than we do," joked Kevin, but soon afterward the regular strokes of currycombs could be heard as Diablo, Sharazan, and Holli were given thorough cleanings.

About twenty minutes later, the animals were standing, saddled, in the yard, and after the kids had tightened the girths, they mounted and rode off happily.

*

The man sat at his desk with a grim expression on his face and stared at the wrinkled piece of paper in his hand. It was a list of addresses. Some were crossed out with red ink, others were circled in blue, and others were followed by large question marks.

"I did this one ... this one ... this one ... this one too. Hmm, those were the most important ones. There won't be much to take from the others." Lost in his thoughts, the man played with a rubber band, rolling it around and around his index fingers. He seemed to be concentrating hard, and while he tried to remember the conversations he had overheard, he went over the things he had already stolen.

"Darn, that's not nearly as much as I had hoped," he mumbled angrily, then crumpled the list and threw the ball of paper against the wall. He slumped over his desk, propped his head up with both hands, and ran his fingers through his hair. In front of him was a newspaper article with a report on a special clinic in Boston.

"I have to find a way to get enough money together to

pay for her operation at this place," he mumbled, the strain of worry showing on his face. And then, exhausted, he let his head fall down onto his arms and closed his eyes. "She just has to get well again." Desperate and bitter, the man cried out loud, "I can't just sit by and watch while my girl becomes paralyzed and has to lie in a bed or sit in a wheelchair for the rest of her life!"

I'll have to make a really large haul, he thought and pulled himself together. *But if I just sit here like a miserable lump, nothing will happen*, he scolded himself.

As he allowed his gaze to wander around the room, his eyes fixed on a large framed photograph of a young, happy girl on a huge black horse. In the background were obstacles for a jumping competition, which the young girl had won.

She looks so happy, thought the man, and at the same time he felt a hatred for the mighty horse, although he knew these feelings weren't justified.

The man's hands trembled as he bent down to pick up the crumpled list of addresses. With a sigh, he unfolded it and once again began to read through the addresses carefully from top to bottom. He thought over the advantages and disadvantages of each single "project," as he called them.

"There's no other way," he concluded after an hour. According to his calculations, he would have to go out again tonight. Time was growing very short.

He went over to the photo and stroked the frame lovingly. "I promise you, sweetheart, we'll make it," he said to the young woman in the photo. Then he turned around abruptly and left the room. There were preparations to be made.

*

Ricki and her friends rode speedily along the narrow path in the woods. Unlike the day before, the horses were now completely relaxed.

"Didn't I tell you that everything would be back to normal?" called Kevin to Ricki.

The girl nodded happily. "That's true! Even the birds are chirping again. But yesterday I thought the world was coming to an end because everything was so quiet."

"Let's ride over to the meadow along the shore," suggested Lillian. "We could take a break there and let the horses drink."

"Good idea," responded Ricki, and decided to wade in the cool water herself, since she hadn't been able to go swimming with the others the day before.

"Can someone hold on to my honey?" she asked a few minutes later, and pressed Diablo's reins into Kevin's hand without waiting for an answer.

"What's up with you?" Bewildered, the boy looked at his girlfriend, who was pulling her feet out of the tall, narrow riding boots with a lot of effort.

"My legs are totally swollen because of the heat," groaned Ricki, and she sighed with relief as the boots finally lay beside her in the grass.

"I'll be right back," she called and marched straight into the cool water of the lake. "Man, that really feels good! Why didn't I think of this before?" She laughed happily and scooped up a handful of water, which she splashed onto her sweaty face. She threw her damp hair back over her shoulders and looked out across Echo Lake as it glistened in the sunlight.

Wow, that is so beautiful, she thought to herself, sensing the familiar happiness that always came over her when she saw the surface of the lake transformed by the sunlight into a sea of millions of sparkling diamonds.

"Hey, Ricki, you're not falling asleep, are you?" Kevin called to her. "Diablo is beginning to miss you!"

"I'm coming!" replied the girl. "Just one more minute." In an effort to keep this fairytale moment in her memory forever, she allowed her gaze to sweep back and forth. Suddenly she was startled by a bright flash on the water's surface.

"What's that?" she murmured and cupped her hands above her eyes so that she could see better. But the bright flash that she thought she'd seen didn't reappear. *I must have been mistaken*, she thought. She shrugged her shoulders and waded back to the shore.

"It's really too bad that the rowboat rental isn't here any-more," commented Lillian. "I can remember it perfectly. When I was six or seven years old, my parents used to bring me here on Sundays, and Dad would row us across the lake. It's only been three years since they decided to forbid boats on the lake ... ever since the nature lovers discovered the rare ducks who live and breed here."

"Good for them! I'm more than willing to give up rowing for the sake of those ducks," answered Ricki.

There! A flash again!

"Hey, am I crazy or is there something floating out there on the lake that's reflecting the sunlight?" she asked everybody and pointed to the spot on the water.

"Where?"

"Well, I don't see anything!"

"Me neither!" said Lillian.

35

Ricki was now having difficulty getting back into her damp, sweaty boots. "Nonsense," she panted with the exertion. "You guys have to look really carefully!"

"I am, but there isn't – Wait! Now I see it, too!" Kevin stared out at the lake. "Well, the first thing that comes to mind is that it's a bottle floating on the surface!"

"A bottle? How could a bottle get out there?"

"Maybe some camper threw it out there? After all, there are plenty of people who get rid of their trash like that!"

"What pigs! They don't care about anything or anybody." Ricki was outraged.

"But that can't be right," concluded Cathy. "If you throw a bottle into the lake from the shore, it floats back to the shore, and the stream that feeds into the lake is much farther down. Therefore, there can't be much of a current here that could pull that thing out so far."

"Wow, that sounds really intelligent!" grinned Lillian.

"Yeah, well, didn't you guys know that I'm a genius? Sometimes I have the feeling that you don't know me at all!" Cathy lifted her eyebrows and pursed her lips, trying to look like a wise old owl.

"If that were a bottle – let's just assume – then it would have to move. But that thing has flashed at least five times and it's still in the same place," reasoned Kevin.

Ricki had managed to pull on her boots at last. "Now all we need is a rowboat in order to solve the mystery of the bottle," she commented.

"Don't tell me you'd really do that?" asked Cathy, astonished.

"Sure I would!" answered Ricki, nodding energetically. "Just imagine, maybe someone left a note in a bottle here –"

"Of course! That's it! A message in a bottle! And in Echo Lake! Probably with a treasure map inside, huh? Ricki, get a grip!" Cathy shook her head.

"No, not a treasure map. I was thinking of something more romantic. Maybe a love letter or something like that."

"I think you've been out in the sun too long, or else you were up late last night watching that sentimental Kevin Costner movie, *Message in a Bottle*, on TV.

Grinning, Ricki took back her horse and swung herself up into the saddle. "And once again, a mystery at Echo Lake has been discovered, which, due to the lack of a rowboat, may never be solved," she recited theatrically, putting her hand across her heart.

"If she goes on like that, she's going to be committed for sure," Cathy exclaimed dryly. Lillian and Kevin immediately positioned their horses next to Diablo.

"What's that supposed to mean? Are you afraid I'm going to fall off my horse, or something?" asked Ricki.

"No, but I think it's better to keep you under control. You never know what you might think of next. You could suddenly make poor Diablo gallop right into the water and head for the bottle, in the hope that an unknown prince sent you a love letter."

Ricki frowned and gazed at her friends pityingly. "Do you all think I'm some kind of lunatic?"

"Never!" protested Lillian, and even Kevin held up his hand as though he were taking an oath.

"You and your ideas," he replied, shaking his head and whispering to Cathy, "The straightjacket! Where did we put the straightjacket?"

Ricki laughed loudly, pressed her calves against Diablo's

belly, and, while her friends stared after her in astonishment, she and Diablo were already rushing along the path in the woods.

"You guys sure are a great escort!" called Ricki laughing. She released the reins a little so that Diablo could increase his speed.

"I think we can forget the straightjacket," grinned Kevin, before he let his Sharazan chase after the black horse.

*

Ricki forgot about the message in a bottle quickly. The gallop on her beloved horse completely took over her thoughts, and once again she gave in to the feeling that there was nothing more wonderful than enjoying the happiness of the moment with Diablo.

Totally lost in her thoughts as she let her horse race around a curve in the path, she was horribly frightened when suddenly a man appeared right in front of them. Screaming loudly, he just saved himself from Diablo's thundering hooves by jumping into the ditch.

"Hey, are you crazy?" the man yelled after Ricki, who had finally been able to halt Diablo a few yards away.

With her face a bright red from embarrassment, she turned her horse around and trotted slowly back to the man, who was leaning over, frantically brushing the fresh dirt off his suit.

"Ruined!" he said between tight lips. "Totally ruined! My dear child, this is going to be expensive!" Only then did he look up.

Seeing Diablo sent cold shivers up and down his spine,

and he took a few steps backward, as though he had suddenly seen a ghost. He got himself under control quickly, however, and then looked at the young rider.

"Oh, Miss Sulai! I should have known! You ride just like you participate in class – completely undisciplined and not paying any attention!"

"Oh, no. Mr. Raymond, I'm really sorry, I didn't see you! I hope you didn't get hurt, did you?" Ricki's face changed colors like a chameleon, from red to white and back to red again.

"We'll talk about this later, young lady! At the latest, in the next history lesson! I guarantee you that you will have so many extra assignments you won't have any time left to ride around so irresponsibly!"

"Uh-oh," responded Kevin, who was able to slow down Sharazan just in time, and in so doing also stop Rashid and Holli, so the man didn't have to jump back into the ditch to avoid being run down. "That looks like trouble," he whispered to Lillian and Cathy, who were staring at their teacher and looking just as worried as Ricki.

"Of all people, it had to be Raymond! Small world," announced Cathy quietly as she regarded Ricki with pity. Ricki was sitting in Diablo's saddle utterly speechless.

After their teacher had vented his anger and continued on his way, Ricki uttered a deep sigh. She realized that from now on she was going to have a tough time with Mr. Raymond, who hadn't liked her much anyway.

With mixed feelings, she started on her way home, her happiness at being in the moment gone up in smoke.

"Let's just hope he doesn't decide to call Mom," a disheartened Ricki said to her friends. "The way she's feeling right now, she might even forbid me from riding my own horse!"

"Oh, come on, Ricki. Don't think like that," Lillian tried to console her. "Mr. Raymond will probably have calmed down by the time he gets home."

"Let's hope so," replied Ricki.

Chapter 3

"Hey, who are those two guys walking around up ahead?" asked Lillian. The friends were on the last leg of their ride back home when they stopped.

Sure enough, they could see two young men coming from the direction of the Sulai farm and just turning onto the road toward the Bates farm.

"I've never seen them before," said Ricki, but when they had ridden closer, Kevin said, "I think I've seen them a few times outside school."

"Are you sure?" Cathy looked over at Kevin doubtfully.

"Nope!" Kevin laughed. "But if it's the two guys I think, then I really do wonder what they're doing here. They seem a little weird. They usually keep to themselves, and they're always ticked off when anyone comes up to them."

"Great! That makes me really glad to see them *leaving* our farm." Ricki stared at the two pensively.

"And what do suppose they want at our place?" Lillian looked at the others questioningly.

"Do I look as if I have a crystal ball?"

"People, somehow I don't think this is our day. Come on,

let's go home." Ricki looked ahead toward the stable, where she thought she could see Jake standing in the doorway.

"I'll bet Jake can tell us what's going on with those two. I have a really funny feeling about all this. Don't ask me why."

"Ricki is having another one of her mysterious moments," grinned Cathy. "Let's hope it's not a bad omen."

*

Jake was waving agitatedly at them, so the kids let their horses trot toward the stable in order to get there sooner, something they didn't usually do.

"Good thing you're finally home," he greeted them and he seemed to be a little upset.

"What's the problem?" Kevin quickly jumped down from Sharazan's saddle.

"Can I take you up on your previous offer?" the old man asked, as he kept changing his stance from one leg to the other.

"Which offer?" Ricki wanted to know, and looked at Jake expectantly.

"To make a long story short," the stable hand began, "I was just at the hospital for a routine examination. You know that my heart hasn't been very strong since my heart attack. Well, anyway, the doctor said that I should stay in the hospital for two days of observation. Apparently he heard some funny noises when he listened to my heart; nothing serious, but enough reason to lock me up in there. I need someone to take care of the animals for two days. Can you kids help me out?"

"Jake, what a question," responded Ricki immediately. "You just make sure that you get healthy again! Don't worry about a thing. We can handle the work around here. After all, we were all instructed in stable maintenance and the care and keeping of horses by a master!" And she gave him a knowing wink.

"Good! Then let me tell your mother right away so that I can get going. My bag is packed and I'm ready to go."

Before he walked to the house, Jake looked at the four teens with affection. "Thanks, kids," he sniffled.

"Good luck, Jake."

"Don't worry. We'll take care of everything."

"Just do what the doctor tells you."

"And get better."

*

Later, when they were unsaddling the horses, Cathy realized that they had completely forgotten to ask Jake about the two strange guys.

"Oh well, if it had been important he would have told us," commented Kevin, and Lillian nodded in agreement.

"Besides, it looks like the two guys walked over to our farm, too. We can probably find out from my parents what it was about."

"Exactly!" Ricki concurred. But just then her mind was not on the two strangers. "Oh, you guys, I hope everything is all right with Jake." Ricki was worried. She really liked the old man. Ever since he had his heart attack and Ricki's dad, Marcus, invited Jake to live with them, she and Harry had adopted him as a surrogate grandfather.

43

"You heard what he said. Those heart noises aren't serious." Kevin shut Sharazan's stall door and went over to his girlfriend to put a comforting hand on her shoulder.

"Says Jake! But we don't know how serious it really is, do we?"

"Please, Ricki, stop it! You've been negative all day!"

"Maybe you're right." Ricki fed Diablo her last carrot and then led him into his stall. "Did you guys read in the paper about the riding accident?" she asked, changing the subject.

"No. What riding accident?" Cathy asked as Lillian and Kevin looked at Ricki expectantly.

"Well, a rider named Lissy Benson had a bad accident at a jumping competition and now she's lying somewhere in a hospital. Supposedly several vertebrae are cracked, she can't move anymore, and no one knows if she'll ever walk again."

"Lissy?!" Lillian was really shocked. Unlike her friends, she knew the talented young rider personally. Four years ago the two girls had been at a riding camp together and had had a lot of fun. While Lillian had taken part in an equestrian workshop, Lissy had finished her jumping training on her beautiful gelding, Tommy Boy.

"The horse had to be put down immediately," Lillian heard Ricki say.

"Oh, no, that's terrible," she whispered, stunned by all this news. "Does anyone know which hospital she's in?"

Ricki shrugged her shoulders. "There was nothing about that in the newspaper. Is Lissy a friend of yours?" she asked tenderly.

"Yeah," answered Lillian, her voice shaky with emotion. She felt her eyes fill with tears. Ricki's words kept echoing

44

in her mind ... *no one knows if she'll ever walk again ... the horse had to be put down immediately.*

"I wonder if she knows that her horse is dead?" Lillian asked softly. "If not, it'll really crush her when she finds out. She loved Tommy Boy more than anything in the world. He was a wonderful animal," Lillian sniffed. "He looked like Diablo ... big, black ... Oh, I feel so sorry for Lissy."

Ricki went over to Lillian and wrapped her arms around her to console her. "I'm sure that Lissy will walk again ... and ... and I'm sure that she'll ride again too," she said as she looked over Lillian's shoulder at Cathy and Kevin, who had grown very quiet.

The friends stood there, realizing that life can change from happy to tragic in a moment, and the lesson made their blood run cold. The fact that Lissy's accident could have happened to any one of them left the four friends speechless.

They walked out of the stable deep in their own thoughts, and a little while later they were all sitting in Ricki's room. But once there, instead of the usual noisy joking around, the mood was somber, and none of the kids could shake their awful feeling.

*

"People in the country really do have more peace and quiet!" commented Richie, after he and his buddy Jack had walked the whole way around the Bates farm without running into anybody at all.

"They don't seem too worried about getting robbed," grinned Jack as he pressed his nose against the window.

"There's an enormous television and an expensive stereo ... I think it would be worth it!"

"Where there are such expensive toys, there's bound to be money lying around, too."

"Maybe under the mattress, or in the linen closet."

Richie and Jack looked at each other, and then looked through the window once more.

"I think we'll have to come back," said Richie, and began walking back in the direction from which they came.

"I think you're right. Look at that enormous horse over there on the paddock. Looks pretty old, doesn't it?" Jack stood still for a moment, thinking.

"Hmm," was all Richie said before he urged Jack to move on. "Hurry up, I have other stuff to do today."

Jack tore himself away from Jonah, and the two young men walked quickly away without noticing Lillian's father. Dave Bates had just stepped out of the barn and was watching them leave, wondering who they were and what they wanted, but they were already too far away for him to bother calling after them.

*

When Ricki arrived at school the next morning on her bike, Lillian, Cathy, and Kevin were already there, waving to her excitedly.

"Good morning, everyone," she called happily, but when she noticed how pale Lillian was, her greeting stuck in her throat.

"What's happened?" she asked and looked from one to the other.

"Josh already called Lillian this morning," Cathy burst out.

"What's up, Lily?" Even Kevin seemed nervous.

Lillian took a deep breath. "Well, as I said, Josh called me really early this morning, while I was still in bed. Last night his father's tack shop was broken into."

"No!" Ricki looked at her friend with astonishment, hardly able to believe what she had heard. "What was stolen?"

Lillian rolled her eyes. "That's the interesting part," she said. "Mr. Cole has some really expensive saddles in the shop. You know, Western saddles with silver trim and stuff. But nothing is missing! Nothing!"

"Are you saying that nothing at all was stolen?" Ricki looked at her a little skeptically.

"Yes, there was! It was the money in the cash register from the day's sales; the one time that Josh's father hadn't taken the money to the bank after closing! The thieves just wanted cash!"

"Who's Josh?" asked Darla Hutchins, one of Lillian's classmates, who was suddenly standing behind her.

"Lillian's boyfriend," Kevin said.

"What? Lillian Bates has a boyfriend? Unbelievable!" Darla grinned at Lillian conceitedly. "He's probably one of those smelly riders, isn't he?"

"A Western-style rider, to be precise," answered Lillian, annoyed. "But you take back that 'smelly rider' crack right now, Darla Hutchins!"

The sixteen-year-old laughed shrilly. "I certainly won't! A Western-style rider? What's the matter, Lillian? Can't you find anyone else? Oh, you country girls," she said with undisguised contempt.

47

Lillian was furious. "Get away from me right now, before I do something I'll regret," she snapped. And with a fake smile, Darla pranced away on her high heels, her rear end swaying back and forth, and headed in the direction of two young men who were leaning against a big maple tree.

"Did you hear that? Lillian has a boyfriend," she giggled as she approached them, poking Jack and Richie in the side. "Who would have thought it? And what a guy! His name is Josh Cole. He's a Western rider, no less."

"Oh, go bother someone else," growled Richie, "We're not interested!" But Jack grabbed Darla by the arm.

"Did you say Cole? Is that the Cole from the tack shop that was broken into last night?" he asked with interest.

"I haven't the faintest idea," complained Doris, bored by this turn in the conversation. And then she walked away in order to tell anyone who would listen about Lillian's boyfriend.

"I hate that witch!" Lillian balled her hands into fists. "What an arrogant bimbo! I'll be so glad when I don't have to see her anymore!"

Just then the school bell rang.

"We've got to hurry up!" exclaimed Ricki, and ran toward her classroom with Cathy and Kevin.

"Well, see you at lunch," the slightly older Lillian shouted to her friends, and then she too had to hurry. Her chemistry teacher hated it when anyone was late to class.

*

"Is this supposed to be a joke, Miss Sulai?" shouted Mr. Raymond nastily, as Ricki handed him her paper. "All you

48

did was copy this word for word out of your history book! You really made it easy on yourself!"

Ricki turned red and got very uncomfortable. If it hadn't been Raymond who had jumped into the ditch to escape Diablo, she would have given him a snappy comeback. She had really worked hard on the paper. Instead, she just ground her teeth together and let him continue to yell at her.

"OK, then we'll do the whole thing over again! Write five pages about Charlemagne for the next class! By the way, he was also a great equestrian," he said sarcastically.

"Five –?" The girl swallowed the rest of the sentence just to be on the safe side.

"Do you have any objections?" Mr. Raymond asked her sharply.

Ricki shook her head slowly and walked back to her seat like a beaten dog.

"So! Then let's focus again on Joan of Arc," announced the teacher and turned to face the blackboard to write down some important dates. He tried to hide his yawn. He hadn't slept well last night.

*

"There's definitely something wrong with him!" Ricki protested when she and her friends met after school let out. "Five pages on Charlemagne?! There isn't that much material in our books. And just who does he think he is? Am I supposed to invent something? You'll see, no matter what and how much I write, it will never be enough for him. He's getting his revenge for being bumped into the ditch."

49

"Come on, Ricki, calm down. If you want, I'll help you this afternoon," Kevin offered.

"Me, too," Cathy joined in and took her friend's arm. "The three of us will get it done in two hours," she said encouragingly.

"I could just kiss both of you!" Ricki sighed with relief. The world didn't look so awful now.

"Charlemagne?" asked Lillian a few minutes later. "Ricki, your day is saved! Two years ago I wrote a paper on him and it has to be lying around somewhere at home."

"Five pages?" asked Ricki cautiously.

Lillian laughed out loud. "My papers were all at least eight pages long!"

Ricki embraced her girlfriend joyfully. "I owe you!" she shouted merrily as she watched Mr. Raymond come down the steps of the school.

"Good bye, Mr. Raymond!" she called boldly, and then she ran over to the bike stand with the others.

The teacher watched her with contempt. "Stupid kid," he mumbled to himself, and then he straightened his shoulders and started to walk away.

*

Incapable of moving, Lissy Benson lay in a sort of plaster cast corset on a special bed. Her head was held in place by a screwed-on devise. If she turned her head even a fraction of an inch, the damaged vertebrae caused a pinching of the spine, a pinch that had already resulted in complete paralysis from the neck down.

Paralyzed, thought the young woman, who was by now

50

resigned to her situation. *I may never walk again, swim again, ride ... ride Tommy Boy again. At least he doesn't have to suffer anymore! Oh, why did I have to jump over that wall? I could tell that the distance wasn't right ... I could have prevented it ... I could have just guided Tommy Boy past it. That wonderful creature had to die because of me, and I ... I'm a cripple forever.* Exhausted and completely burned out, the young woman closed her eyes.

In shock after the accident, Lissy had repeatedly demanded to see the video her father had taken of her performance at the last horse show. It was a jumping event, and she had won it by a big lead astride Tommy Boy.

"I don't think that would be a good idea," the doctor had said gravely. "It would be too upsetting for her to see herself completely healthy, especially riding on her beloved horse."

But her father rejected the doctor's well-intentioned advice.

"Believe me, doctor, I know my daughter. And if anything can strengthen her resolve to heal, it'll be seeing herself – a prize-winning, capable, *strong* rider – on this video."

"But the horse –" objected the doctor again.

"To see Tommy Boy, to watch him again and again, will help her deal with his death." Lissy's father breathed deeply. "My daughter is stronger than you think," he said softly.

The doctor looked fixedly at the broken man sitting in front of him, and searched for a way to comfort him.

"Perhaps it would be worth a try. Quite often shocks are successfully treated with counter-shocks," he said slowly. "Where is this video?"

With trembling fingers, Lissy's father searched for the video in the shopping bag he had brought with him.

Embarrassed, he handed it to the doctor across the desk, and the medical man understood that this father would have granted his daughter's request whether he, as her doctor, had approved of it or not.

"You love your daughter very much, don't you?" the doctor asked softly.

"More than my life," whispered Lissy's father. "If I could, I would change places with her right now. She has her whole life ahead of her. It's so unfair that I, at my age, could easily run an obstacle course, while she, at seventeen, will be confined to a bed for the rest of her life. What was God thinking? What in the world was he thinking?" he repeated in despair and stared in his helplessness at the doctor, as though he could give him the answer to his question.

"What I have learned from my practice of medicine is that there are many things that we humans – smart and clever as we are – will never be able to understand," said Dr. Kennedy before getting up. "And now let's hope that you are right about your daughter and that video."

*

Lissy watched the video over and over again and dreamed that she was back in the past, before the accident. Finally she understood that she was lying to herself, and asked the nurse to turn off the TV.

Today was the first day that she just lay there with her eyes closed, with no thoughts at all. A yawning emptiness had overtaken her, and even the senselessness of her future motionless life didn't fill her with dread anymore. She had given up and, because of her guilt in the death of Tommy

Boy, was willing to accept her fate as a cripple, as she called herself, without complaint.

The door to Lissy's room was ajar, and she could hear several faint voices talking in the corridor outside her room.

"Mr. Alcott? Well, for heaven's sake, what are you doing here?" one of the nurses asked.

"One of your doctors insisted on examining my old pump, and now I have to stay here for two whole days, although I have a lot to do at home!" complained Jake. But it was obvious that he was glad to see that the nurse had remembered him.

"Well, then you're on the wrong floor. Your room would be one floor above this one," said Mae Liang in her gentle voice. She took the old man's elbow tenderly.

"Say, couldn't you put in a few good words for me, so that I can get out of here?" he asked, winking. Mae Liang just smiled at him.

"I'm sorry, but – " At that moment the red light went on over Lissy's door. "Excuse me, Mr. Alcott, but I'm afraid I'm going to have to leave you now. I have to answer that red light, but we'll see each other soon, I'm sure," the nurse said, pleasantly, and then she turned into Lissy's room. "Lissy, what's up?" she asked in an especially cheery voice.

"Nurse Mae, who was that just now? Outside the door?"

"Who do you mean, Lissy?"

"The man with whom you were just speaking."

"Oh, Mr. Alcott? He's a very nice older gentleman, who –"
Jake, who was always extremely curious, had followed Mae Liang to the door and had risked a glance at the young woman who, as though she were being tortured, lay attached to her bed.

Poor girl, he thought. Carefully, he pushed the door open a little wider and stared at the patient.

"Lissy? Lissy Benson? Heavens! What happened to you?" Uninvited, Jake now came bursting into the room and looked in shock at the young woman.

Mae Liang started to push the old man out of the room when Lissy opened her eyes.

"Jake!" A sad smile appeared on her pale face. "It's great to see you again," she said softly, as the stable hand freed himself from Nurse Mae's grip, pulled up a chair to the bed, and sat down without being asked.

Slowly he let his gaze travel over Lissy's body, and felt his eyes begin to burn.

My goodness, what in the world happened? he thought, as his memory took him back to his first meeting with the girl.

Lissy, who was thirteen years old at the time, had participated in a workshop on jumping with her horse at the Summersfield Ranch, where Jake was then working. And, like all the other young riders there, she would always come in the evenings to listen to his stories. They were fun weeks, but also very tiring. Every day the kids would cook up new pranks to torment Jake with.

"Lissy, child," whispered the old man, and he felt his heart break as Lissy said, almost tonelessly, "Tommy is dead ... and it was my fault."

Tommy Boy? Jake's face twitched. "Don't talk, Lissy. Everything's going to be all right," he said hoarsely and then stood up abruptly as Mae Liang gestured to him.

"I'll be back, little one. Don't worry ... I –"

"Please, Mr. Alcott, leave now!" The nurse pushed him forcefully toward the door.

54

"What happened here?" asked Jake, his voice heavy with concern.

"A riding accident. Several cracked vertebrae and probable paralysis. I'm sorry, but you're not family, and I'm not supposed to give you any information. But take care, Mr. Alcott. I'll try to keep you up to date when I can."

"Paralyzed." Suddenly Jake felt as though his knees were going to buckle. With shuffling steps and drooping shoulders, he moved slowly along the hospital corridor to the elevator, and was glad when he finally reached his room and could just let himself fall onto the bed.

"Oh dear, oh dear," Jake's roommate complained loudly, and he pressed his hand on the bandage that was wrapped around his backside. They had operated on a boil there a few days before. "It still hurts!"

"Oh, be quiet," Jake yelled at the whining man. "You have no idea what it feels like to be really sick!"

"Well, excuse me!" the patient shot back, forgetting his pain temporarily over his anger at Jake's words.

"I don't excuse anything!" growled Jake. "But since I'm supposed to recuperate here, I'll ask you to keep your mouth shut, otherwise, it's possible that I might kick you in your sore behind and take you to the bedside of a sweet seventeen-year-old girl who will probably be paralyzed for the rest of her life! So be quiet, and be glad that you're so healthy!"

Without another word, the man let himself fall back onto the pillow. *I'm sharing my room with a crazy person*, he thought, and decided it would be better to keep his mouth shut. Everyone knew that one shouldn't provoke crazy people.

Chapter 4

Josh had ridden on Cherish, his small piebald mare, to meet the four friends after school. "Hey, everybody!" He casually tapped the cowboy hat he always wore when he was riding. It was, after all, the traditional headgear of a Western rider.

"Hello, Josh! Everything OK?" Kevin wanted to ask about the burglary the previous evening at Josh's father's riding shop, but he could see that Lillian's boyfriend had something else on his mind.

"Well, sweetie," Josh said to Lillian as he bent down from his saddle and gave her a tender kiss on the cheek, "we haven't seen each other in a while, have we?"

Lillian nodded and sighed. "Three whole days! Almost an eternity!"

"Listen to all this lovey-dovey talk. It's unbearable!" groaned Cathy, and she rolled her eyes.

"You're just jealous!" commented Josh, which made the girl blush a little. He wasn't very far off.

"Nonsense – total nonsense!"

"Why are you blushing, then? By the way, are people allowed to go rowing on Echo Lake again?"

"Wouldn't that be great? These days, you'd be lucky to paddle around on an inner tube without getting a warning. Why do you ask?" Kevin was curious.

"Well, first, I came across a rowboat today –"

Ricki grinned. "Tell us, how does one find a boat like that?"

"Just let me finish. I was riding along the shore on Cherish when my cell phone rang –"

"What? You have your cell phone on when you're riding? How unromantic!"

"Yeah, well, after the burglary last night, it could have been someone from the police station who needed a statement from me. In which case it would be really practical if they could reach me, wouldn't it? So! Do you want to know where the boat was?"

"Of course!"

"Good, now where *was* I? Oh, yeah, well, my cell phone rang, and as I was trying to fish it out of my backpack, it slid out of my hand and fell down the bank of the lake. I dismounted and crawled down the slope on all fours, and what do you know? There it was! It was hidden under branches and brush, so you couldn't see it from either the path or the lakeside."

"Your phone?" Ricki teased.

Josh rolled his eyes. "The boat, you idiot! Are you trying to drive me crazy, or are you really that stupid?"

"Neither," replied Ricki, deadly serious. "And then what happened?"

"Then I saw a really strange guy walking around there who definitely didn't make a good impression on me."

"And you think that weird guys automatically hide rowboats on Echo Lake, is that it?" remarked Kevin.

"You know what, just forget it! Everything's a joke to you people. It's impossible to have a normal conversation with you guys. Lillian, are you sure you should be hanging out with these kids?"

"Absolutely! Come on, let's ride over to the spot you just described. Maybe there are more mysteries to be solved," she responded and turned Holli in the direction of Echo Lake. The others followed her. Maybe there was an adventure ahead.

*

"It's over there," called Josh after a while, and pointed to a rather tangled slope on the shore.

"Wow, someone found a great hiding place. Do you guys have any idea how much I'd like to row across the lake?" Lillian's eyes began to glow with anticipation.

"Lily, you have some wild ideas!" Ricki, who seemed to be able to read her friend's mind, raised her finger in warning.

"A row in the moonlight, probably, with Josh at the oars, or something like that. Is that what you have in mind?" Cathy asked, shaking her head, a look of disgust on her face.

"Yeah, I admit, that's about how I imagined it!"

"What did you say about a full moon?" asked Kevin.

"What do you mean?"

"Well, honestly, a boat ride at night by full moon would appeal to me, too," he grinned, and it looked as though a forbidden boat trip was starting to tempt the kids.

Meanwhile, Diablo, who was getting bored with just

standing around, started scraping the dirt with his hoof, making small clumps of grass fly off to the side.

"Diablo doesn't like standing still for so long. Let's keep riding," said Ricki, who was glad when the others nodded in agreement.

"We can talk while we're riding! Look back there." Ricki peered into the woods. "Aren't those the two guys who were hanging around near my house yesterday?"

"You're seeing ghosts, Ricki! There's nobody there! But if you want, we can ride over there and look around," offered Kevin. Ricki just waved his suggestion aside.

"No, I don't feel like chasing after ghosts! I'd rather discuss whether we should go on a moonlight party on the lake or not!"

While the kids rode happily along the shore, they were followed by angry glances.

"They're always around at the wrong time," mumbled the shady character who was hiding near the rowboat. "It's time to finish this thing!"

*

Richie and Jack had turned off the main path and were making their way through the dense brush.

"Sometimes I wonder why we're doing all this," said Richie, jerking his bag free from the tangled branches.

"Be careful, darn it," complained Jack quietly. "If you lose half of that stuff, it'll all have been for nothing, and I have absolutely no desire to get yelled at by Langdon. I wouldn't put it past him to send us out for weeks at a time."

59

Richie nodded. "I'll be glad when we're done with all this. It could get dangerous."

"When are we going to do those farms?"

"I have no idea. Let's do it when it fits into our schedule."

"And when will it fit into our schedule?"

"Man, you're getting on my nerves! Let's go out tonight sometime. That should finish it, and satisfy Langdon!" whispered Richie as he crawled deeper and deeper into the brush.

*

"Hey, look, there's something flashing in the same spot I saw it yesterday!" Ricki called out as she stared out across the surface of Echo Lake.

"You're right!" Kevin rode Sharazan nearer to the shore. "It looks like it hasn't moved. Do you think it could be a buoy, or something like that?"

"There are buoys only on the other end of the lake, where the breeding ground for the ducks is sectioned off," explained Josh. "Anyway, buoys have green and yellow stripes and are much larger!"

"Maybe it's a bottle after all. There has to be an explanation for that flashy thing out there," insisted Ricki.

"Hey, I have a great idea," said Lillian, excited by her own cleverness. "Why don't we just row out there tonight and take a look?"

"Are you crazy? If the park ranger catches us, we'll really be in trouble!" Cathy felt uncomfortable with the idea of a nighttime excursion.

"You don't really think he has time to patrol the lake at

night, to see if anyone's rowing on it, do you, Cathy?" Lillian turned back to Ricki.

"Well, what do you think? Should we do this or shouldn't we?" Lillian wanted to know, but before Ricki could give her an answer, Josh asked, a little confused, "Hey, what's this really about? Do you guys want to go count buoys or what?"

"No," laughed Kevin. "Ricki thinks that she spotted a bottle with a message inside, and she won't give up until she finds out what's really out there floating in the lake."

"Oh!"

"Let's do it!" Ricki nodded at Lillian conspiratorially. "I think if I don't find out what that thing is, I'll go crazy."

"Remember what happened to the curious cat!" grinned Kevin. "But, to be honest, I'm beginning to get curious about the secret of Echo Lake, too!"

"Well, then, we're agreed! Now all we have to do is convince our parents that a moonlight boat ride on this beautiful night is absolutely necessary for our inner happiness."

"Exactly! And since tomorrow is Saturday, and Ricki already cleaned up her room, it might just work!" Lillian glanced once more at the middle of the lake before turning Doc Holliday around.

"Well, *my* mother would have a fit if she heard anything about a night ride! She had enough of night rides the last time, when Ricki and Kevin were missing all night." Cathy urged Rashid forward next to Diablo, who was slowly trotting behind Holli.

"We'll just have to make her understand that we have Josh with us to protect us and watch out for danger. You *are* coming with us, aren't you?" Lillian looked pleadingly at her boyfriend.

61

"Of course. For stuff like this, I'm your man!"

"Great! See, Cathy, now we have an argument that'll persuade your mother!"

"Could be, but I'm not sure. Well, if worse comes to worse, you can tell me tomorrow how it went!"

The kids rode back home as quickly as possible to make preparations for their nighttime outing. When they had left the woods, Josh separated himself from the rest of the group.

"Let's talk on the phone later to pick a meeting place and to make sure everything's all set. See you," he said and waved good-bye to Lillian.

"Later!" the others shouted, and then they let their horses trot along the old country road.

In their minds, they all saw themselves sitting in the little boat as the full moon reflected romantically on the water, losing its light in the water rings where the oars dipped into the lake.

*

"And there's nothing else that can be done?" Jake stared gravely at Dr. Kennedy.

Sighing, the doctor shrugged his shoulders. "My dear Mr. Alcott, if Lissy hadn't told you the whole story during your second, and by the way, forbidden, visit with her, I wouldn't tell you anything about this anyway. I hope you know that."

"Yeah, yeah, doctor, don't drag this out any more than necessary. Lissy said that there aren't any doctors locally who could perform the operation, or who'd even dare risk it. But isn't it your duty to at least try? After all, the child is only seventeen years old! You can't just say you're afraid to try!"

"Please don't attempt to explain to me what we as doctors should or should not risk. I don't try to give you any tips on how you should take care of your horses. I have as little knowledge of horses, Mr. Alcott, as you have about operations!"

Jake held up his hands to ease the tension.

"I didn't mean to attack you personally, Doctor, but I think ... I wanted ..."

Dr. Kennedy looked at his watch and stood up. "Unfortunately, I don't have any more time to discuss medical procedures with you. Just know that if we operate, there is a risk that the young woman will be paralyzed from the neck down if even the most minimal complication occurs during the operation. As she is now, there is at least the possibility that only her legs will be paralyzed, and she will still have the use of her hands and arms. Now, I don't want to discuss this with you any further."

Jake had listened without saying a word. The thought that the carefree girl he had met on the Summersfield Ranch would have to sit in a wheelchair for the rest of her life sent him into a deep depression.

"For heaven's sake," he thundered. "There must be a doctor somewhere who –"

"Somewhere, of course, Mr. Alcott, but not here!" Dr. Kennedy interrupted Jake's outburst. "Please, believe me, if I could, then –"

"Boston!" Jake shouted, practically overturning his chair as he stood up. "I read in some magazine article that there are specialists there who –"

"Mr. Alcott! Please! Even if there were such a doctor there, the girl shouldn't be moved! Even the slightest jolt could damage her spinal cord permanently!"

"Then the doctor has to come here!"

Sighing, the doctor leaned against his desk. "Do you know what it costs to fly in a specialist? And do you have any idea how much money an operation like that would cost? The insurance companies pay only a fraction of what the doctor's fee would be! It's just unaffordable, and then ... the risk, which I just explained to you, remains, nevertheless! No one can guarantee that Lissy Benson will be completely cured after the operation! Do you understand? Now I really have to go!" Dr. Kennedy opened the door and waited for Jake to leave his office.

Once again the old man took a breath, about to say something, but then changed his mind. Without saying another word, he bowed his head and shuffled past the doctor. But outside the office, he stopped and turned to face the doctor.

"I understand," he growled. "Money is more important to people than health! What kind of a cruel world do we live in?"

Dr. Kennedy rolled his eyes, took a deep breath, and was glad when Jake finally left. Pensively, he watched the old man walk away and then he closed the door more loudly than he had intended.

For one moment Dr. Kennedy stared straight ahead, furious. *Good heavens, he's right!* the doctor thought to himself. *He's so right!* Then he went back to his desk with a determined air. He stared at his telephone before he picked up the receiver and pressed the button for his secretary.

64

"Emily, please, connect me with Doctor Tom Albright in Boston. I believe you have his number on file. He's at Mass General Hospital. And don't let them try to get rid of you! Tell them anything, but make sure that I get him on the line. Yes, immediately! Good, thank you!"

Slowly he put down the receiver. No one was going to accuse him of not doing everything in his power to save that vital young girl from a life in a wheelchair – especially not a stubborn old stable hand like Jake!

Dr. Kennedy smiled. *He reminds me of my grandfather*, he thought as he attached his beeper to the pocket of his coat and left to begin his rounds to see patients.

*

"Oh no, Ricki. Don't think for a minute that I'll let you go on a nighttime ride, especially when there won't be any adults with you! We've already been through one terrible night ride! No! Absolutely not!" Brigitte turned away from her daughter and started to put away the clean breakfast and lunch dishes that were in the dish drain. The fear for her daughter's safety that she had felt a few months earlier when Ricki had been separated from the rest of the group during a storm to search for Kevin was always with her. *I just can't go through that anxiety again*, she said to herself.

"But Mom, Lillian's parents are letting her go, and Cathy just called to say it was OK with her mother as long as Josh is going too. And Kevin –"

"Ricki, I said NO! Lillian is almost sixteen, Kevin is fifteen. Cathy isn't, but she's not my daughter. Josh is seventeen and probably makes his own decisions about what he does or doesn't do, but he isn't an adult yet either. You are NOT going to go riding at night! Do you understand me? It's enough that I'm scared to death every time you go riding during the day, but at night –"

Tears filled Ricki's eyes. "I was really looking forward to it, and now –"

"Then find something else to look forward to! You're staying home! End of discussion!" Brigitte left the kitchen in order to avoid any more argument, but she knew that Ricki probably wouldn't speak to her for at least two days.

"Darn, darn, darn!" Ricki stamped her foot on the floor and threw the glass that she had been holding into the sink, where it shattered. "Way to go, Ricki! Great! Really fantastic!" Hands trembling with fury, she began to pick the glass shards out of the sink.

"Ouch, darn it!" Quickly she turned on the cold water and held her bleeding finger under the faucet while she searched for a bandage in the drawer with the other hand.

"How come you're letting the water run so long?" asked Harry, who had just come through the door.

"Just leave me alone!" Ricki snapped at her little brother and slammed the drawer shut with a bang.

"Why are you so mad?"

Ricki's eyes were flashing, but she didn't say a word. It wasn't Harry's fault that she wasn't allowed to go riding tonight with the others.

Silently, she wrapped her cut finger in a bunch of paper towels, then, much more carefully than before, she collected the rest of the broken glass and threw it into the garbage can before she rushed out of the room.

Harry watched her leave in bewilderment. "Sisters are

weird!" he mumbled to himself, and then he grabbed a tablespoon and went for the Rocky Road ice cream he remembered was in the freezer.

"Hmm, delicious." He smacked his lips happily and didn't stop eating until he heard steps in the hallway.

*

Ricki had taken her cell phone with her into the stable and now she called all of her friends to tell them the bad news.

"Oh well, Ricki, it isn't the end of the world." Lillian tried to console her, but it didn't work.

"I was looking forward to it so much, but Mom's acting so bizarre right now. I don't know what's wrong with her. She's always in a bad mood. And I really thought we were finally going to solve the riddle of the message in a bottle today."

"But we don't even know if that shiny thing *is* a bottle! Maybe it's something completely different, and −"

"It doesn't matter anyway!" Ricki cut her off. "I just wanted to go along on the moonlight ride. The bottle is secondary."

Diablo stretched his head way above the stable walls and nudged Ricki's shoulder.

"Hey, you, stop it!"

"What should I stop?" asked Lillian, confused.

"Oh, not you! Diablo is nibbling at me!" Ricki laughed, but then she stopped the conversation abruptly. "I'll call you later," she said to Lillian. "A taxi just drove up and, if I'm not mistaken, Jake is inside. Later." She shut off her cell phone and ran outside.

"Jake, what are you doing here? I thought you weren't coming back until tomorrow," she called to him as she opened the taxi door.

"Hi, Ricki. I just took off!" the old man grinned and pulled out his wallet to pay the taxi driver.

"How come?" asked the girl, astonished as she reached for Jake's bag.

"I just realized that I'm not half as sick as some other people, and anyway, you can't get well in a hospital. What you see and hear there doesn't exactly help you to heal!"

"Oh!"

"Are the horses OK?" Jake wanted to know as he walked straight to the stable.

"Jake, you were only gone one day!" Ricki reminded him.

"One day is enough to turn the world completely upside down," the old man replied and greeted each animal as though he had just returned from a trip around the world.

*

Josh took it on himself to try to change Mrs. Sulai's mind about the nighttime ride. Late in the day, he arrived at the Sulai farm on his bike to put in a good word for Ricki. Kevin, Cathy, and Lillian, whom he had called, were there to back him up.

"Please, Mrs. Sulai," he began politely. "It's still summer, and it stays light out until at least eight o'clock. Couldn't we ride at dusk? After all, there's no storm brewing, and the full moon will light up the whole area. Nobody's going to wind up in a ditch. Please, Mrs. Sulai. There's nothing nicer than going for a walk or a ride in the moonlight on a mild evening," he said winking.

"Why don't you just *walk* around the lake?" snapped Brigitte.

"We're horseback riders, Mrs. Sulai!" explained Josh simply.

"And anyway, Ricki is our best friend, and without her it just won't be any fun," Cathy added, cautiously, and got an annoyed glance from her friend's mother for her trouble.

"Then don't go," was Brigitte's equally simple answer.

"This isn't going to work!" Kevin whispered to Lillian, "I think she really is mad ... ultra mad, I'd say!"

"What's going on with you guys?" asked Jake, who had just stepped outside his cottage and was observing the group in the yard with surprise.

"I have forbidden my daughter to participate in another nighttime ride because I'm still not over the last one, but that doesn't seem to interest anybody here!"

"We don't want to go riding at midnight just in the evening, when it starts to get dark. Along Echo Lake, because we thought that it would be really beautiful with the full moon," explained Kevin, and Jake grinned at him like a coconspirator.

"Extremely beautiful, especially when the girlfriends are along, isn't it?" he asked, and Kevin and Josh nodded enthusiastically.

"Jake! Ricki is still only thirteen!" Brigitte shook her head.

"Excuse me, Mrs. Sulai, but Ricki's going to be fourteen soon," Kevin corrected her cautiously.

"I know when my daughter's birthday is!"

69

"Oh, let them have their fun, Brigitte." Jake was still thinking about Lissy, who would probably never have any such wonderful experiences again. "Today's generation is more mature than we were at their age, and anyway, I'm sure that the boys will take good care of the girls, won't they?"

"Of course!"

"Absolutely!"

"Oh, please, Mrs. Sulai," began Cathy again.

Brigitte looked slowly from one child to another, and although her misgivings hadn't abated, she nodded. "Oh, all right. You'll do what you want to do with or without my OK. So go ahead."

"Does that mean I'm allowed to go?" asked Ricki, still a little unsure.

"Yes, but only if you're back by nine o'clock at the latest. No later!"

"Yeahhhh!" Happy and relieved, the kids hugged each other, and Ricki gave Jake a kiss on the cheek.

"Thanks, Jake. You're the greatest!"

"You don't have to shout at me."

"Sorry, but I'm so happy," Ricki called out as she ran into the stable with her friends. "Diablo, we're going on a full-moon ride!" she informed her black horse immediately and loudly. He just gave her a surprised look as she danced around excitedly in front of his stall.

*

"Hello, Tom, how are you?" Dr. Kennedy said cordially into the receiver.

"Ah, Phillip, old boy, I'm well, thanks. To what do I owe the pleasure of your call? Are you having problems, or do you need somewhere to stay because you're giving lectures in Boston again? You know, there's always room for you here with Betty and me."

Dr. Kennedy could see the impish smile of his old friend and colleague in his mind's eye.

"Tell Betty I said hello, but she won't have the pleasure of my company this time. No, no, I'm calling for a completely different reason ... We have a complicated case here, and I thought maybe you could help us."

Dr. Albright became serious immediately. "Tell me about it, and don't leave out any details, please," he said, and listened silently and with total concentration as his friend explained.

"That does sound complicated," Albright said after he heard Dr. Kennedy's description of the case. "You know that I never make a diagnosis over the phone. I'll have to see the young lady for myself and examine her. But you already said that she shouldn't be moved."

"Tom, I know it's asking a lot, but could you come here?"

"Phillip, I could get into a lot of trouble if I started a treatment there that hasn't been given the OK from my superiors, especially a treatment this complex."

"Do you see any chance of a cure?"

"As I already said, I don't make long-distance diagnoses. But, Phil, there is always a chance, even if it's only a small one."

"So, you'll come?" Dr. Kennedy held his breath.

"I'm sure I can come up with a good excuse for the trip,"

Dr. Albright answered quietly. "I'll call you. Take care, old friend."

"Thank you," murmured Lissy's doctor as he hung up the phone, satisfied that he'd done his best for his young patient. "If Tom Albright really does come, you have a chance, Lissy," he said aloud, though there was no one to hear him.

Chapter 5

"Thanks for backing me up, guys. I can't tell you how happy I am that Mom finally relented," Ricki crowed as she cleaned Diablo from head to hoof. "When should we leave?"

"Josh said he'd be at the Echo Lake parking lot at eight o'clock. That means we should leave about seven-thirty," yelled Kevin from Sharazan's stall.

"And he's bringing some stuff to eat!" Lillian announced, peering on tiptoe over Doc Holliday's high back.

"Great! And when are we going to go rowing?" asked Cathy in a loud voice.

"Shhh! Be quiet! Don't tell the whole world! If my mom gets wind of it, I can forget the ride!" Ricki glanced at her girlfriend angrily.

Cathy hunched down. "Sorry, I didn't think of that!" she whispered apologetically.

"What time is it now?"

"Six forty-five."

"Good, then we don't really need to hurry that much. Guys, I am so excited!" Ricki put her currycomb and brush aside and then stood behind Diablo, watching him from the side.

"Are you thinking of untangling his tail, too?" asked Lillian. "It'll be almost dark when we leave. No one's going to see how good he looks."

"That's true, but I can't just stand around doing nothing until it's time to leave."

"Well, do you kids already have full-moon fever?" Jake asked as he came through the stable door.

"Of course! Hey, Jake, what did the doctor say? Are you OK?" Kevin said as he came out of the stall and went over to the old man.

"Doctors," Jake grunted with contempt. "What do they know? Of course I'm OK! But there's a young girl at the hospital, Lissy –"

Lillian perked up her ears. "Lissy? Lissy Benson?" she asked, upset, and came out into the corridor as well.

Jake nodded. "That's the one! Do you know her? She had a –"

"A bad riding accident, yeah, I know," Lillian interrupted. "She was at the hospital where you had your tests? Tell me, Jake, how's she doing?" Lillian swallowed nervously.

"It doesn't look good. The doctor tells me they're afraid to operate," he said solemnly.

The kids looked at each other, visibly upset.

"So it's really as bad as the story in the newspapers said?" Lillian wanted to know.

"I think it's even worse!" answered Jake.

"Can she have visitors?" asked Lillian, whose joy over the moonlight ride was now clouded by Lissy's health problems.

"I don't know," Jake shrugged. "I just barged in without

asking anyone's permission. The nurse and the doctor weren't too pleased with me, but at least I got a smile out of the girl. I know her from a long time ago."

"Yeah, me too." Lillian looked sad.

"Well, if I were you, I'd just go there. I'm sure she'd really be glad to see you. And happiness is the best medicine, isn't it?"

"But if you say that she's –" Lillian went silent. She didn't want to utter the awful word "paralyzed" out loud.

"Listen, child, why don't you all just go riding now, and tomorrow you can decide if you want to visit Lissy or not. But if you do go, don't go with that sad expression on your face. Bring her joy and laughter and enthusiasm. That's what she needs right now."

"Yes, Jake, I understand." Lillian tried to smile, but she wasn't quite able to pull it off.

"We should probably get the horses ready," announced Ricki, and she put her hand gently on Lillian's shoulder. "If you want, we could all go with you to visit your friend."

Lillian nodded gratefully. "That would be great," she whispered hoarsely, and slowly she walked back to Holli to saddle him. Lissy was very much in her thoughts, and her friends' support was a great comfort. *Sometimes they can be an irritating bunch*, she had to admit to herself, *but they're always there when I need 'em.*

*

The dark-clad figure of a man slipped unnoticed between the stately homes of the wealthy businesspeople in town. Cited on large, beautifully landscaped lots, the homes lined both sides of Main Street, the town's major thoroughfare. The man seemed nervous and disoriented in the semidarkness, but didn't dare risk using his flashlight. He stumbled and fell, knocking over a garbage can. *Any second now*, he thought, *the clanging of alarms is going to bring the whole neighborhood to the street. I'll never get in there! I'm much too early anyway.*

Lights went on outside one of the homes and bathed part of the front yard in bright light. Startled, the man remained frozen with fear on the ground for a fraction of a second before he jumped up and ran away.

It has to end ... there has to be an end. I can't go on like this. If they catch me it all will have been for nothing. Panting, he rushed off, leaving the residential area behind him. Darn! He'd forgotten about the full moon.

*

"So, our countdown begins," Richie whispered as he and Jack walked the familiar path through the woods around Echo Lake. They were dressed in dark clothing, and as they moved slowly among the trees they were almost impossible to see.

"Langdon will be satisfied when we give him our loot tomorrow morning."

"If not, he can go and get the eggs himself next time!"

The two of them struggled through the undergrowth and bushes.

"We were really lucky that we discovered that stuff. Do you think we'll be able to get it out of the water OK?" asked Jack, wiping the sweat from his forehead.

76

"Nothing's for sure in this line of work!" replied Richie. "The important thing is that we be really quiet. One sound from us and it's all over!"

Jack nodded, although his buddy, who was walking in front of him, couldn't see him. Somehow the young man was glad that, starting tomorrow, he could spend his nights in bed again.

*

"There they are!" Josh stood next to Cherish and peered in the direction of the old country road. The outline of his friends, accompanied by the swaying beams of light from two flashlights, appeared in the fading evening light.

"Have you been waiting long?" asked Lillian, who had ridden ahead.

"No, no. Is everything OK with you and your mom, Ricki?"

"Happily, yes!"

"OK, then, let's get going! And let's hope no one has borrowed the rowboat tonight," laughed Josh as he swung himself quickly onto Cherish's saddle. "I hope you guys like chicken sandwiches," he said as the group got underway.

*

Completely drained and trembling with fear, the would-be burglar had fled the residential area on foot and made his way to the entrance to Echo Lake. Looking about him to make sure he hadn't been followed, he leaned against a tree trunk to catch his breath. He put his hand on his right knee, which had started to hurt a lot, and then forced himself to keep going.

No one can ever find out what I've done, he said to himself with determination. Then he pulled himself together and turned onto the little path that would lead him, indirectly, to the old rowboat, which he had planned to send to the bottom of Echo Lake after his last trip tonight. Once that was done, all his tracks would be erased.

He found the boat easily in the cove where he had beached it earlier and was just removing the camouflaging branches when he suddenly stopped short. *That's impossible*, went through his mind, and he was filled with fear as he heard quiet whispering and soft laughter, accompanied by the sounds of footsteps.

Feet? No, it's something else.

The rustling sounds and muted voices grew louder.

Darn it, who can be here at this time of night? He glanced at the boat, trying to decide whether to re-cover it or not, but then he realized that it was more important that he hide himself until the people – whoever they were – were gone. He would have to postpone his plans for scuttling the rowboat. He found a hiding place under the overhanging branches of a willow tree along the shoreline and, up to his ankles in water, waited.

I hope they go soon, he prayed, starting to shiver.

*

"I think it was somewhere around here," Josh said, bringing Cherish to a halt. "But at night everything looks so different."

78

"Well, I probably wouldn't have been able to find it right away either." Cathy jumped down from Rashid's back and yawned behind her hand.

"Don't tell me you're tired," laughed Ricki and poked her friend in the ribs.

"I seem to be," admitted the girl.

"So, here we are! What now? Ready to row out and fight the rough seas in order to free the genie in Ricki's bottle?" Kevin, always the smart-Alec, hadn't kept his voice down, and the man hiding under the willow branches heard his words loud and clear.

For one panicky moment he was tempted, regardless of the danger, to flee. If there was one thing that couldn't happen, it was that these kids should discover his secret.

Stay calm, the man pleaded with himself as he tried to control his chattering teeth. He was wet, cold, and scared to death.

"Sure, but what should we do with the horses?" asked Ricki as she stroked Diablo's neck lovingly.

Horses! Of course. Those weren't feet I heard; they were hooves. I should have realized it sooner. It's those kids who are always hanging around the lake with their nags! Hurry up and leave! Come on, leave ... leave ... leave. But his silent pleading was to no avail.

"The boat is too small for all of us," observed Lillian. "I suggest we go in two groups. Josh, Cathy, and I could paddle around for fifteen minutes or so while you take care of our horses, and then you two can go and visit the mysterious bottle while we take care of Diablo and Sharazan."

"That's exactly what we'll do! Great idea." Kevin nodded in approval.

"Or do you guys want to go first?" Lillian asked.

"It doesn't matter, but since Josh discovered the boat, you guys go first."

"First we'd better find out if the thing is still there. And that there are oars." Josh handed Cherish's reins to Lillian. "I'll be right back!"

"I hope so much that this works out," Ricki whispered to Kevin. "Or else that whole scene with Mom will have been for nothing."

"Let's wait and see!"

Anxiously the kids stared at the opening in the trees through which Josh had disappeared down to the shoreline.

"Well, this is odd," they heard him say when he reappeared a few minutes later. "The boat is almost completely uncovered. Someone must have uncovered it hastily – and recently. Look what I found." Josh held up a little flashlight in the shape of a pen and let the beam shine through the darkness.

"How do you know that hasn't been lying around for a while?" asked Kevin, and stepped nearer in order to examine the little tool more closely.

"It was under the seat – it probably rolled under – and it was still on!"

"No! Wow! Now this is getting interesting!"

"It could have been on for a while," suggested Cathy, but Josh shook his head firmly.

"The light's very strong. If it had been on for a long time, the battery would have run down and the light would be faint!"

"You should work for the FBI," joked Ricki as she shifted her weight from one leg to the other impatiently. "You know what? I don't care about the silly flashlight. Were there oars or paddles in the boat?"

Josh nodded. "Yeah, but I'm not sure it would be a good idea to row across the lake when the owner of the boat could be nearby."

"To be honest, it seems a little too risky to me, too." Cathy looked worried. She had a premonition that something was going to go wrong tonight.

"Well, I'm sure that we would have already gotten in trouble if someone were still close by. I can't imagine anybody being stupid enough to watch us get in his boat and row away without saying something."

"True! OK. Who goes first?"

"Let's do it like we decided earlier!"

"Good! Lily, come on! And Cathy –" Josh reached out his hand, but the girl shook her head slowly.

"I think I'll pass and stay here with the horses. I've got a bad feeling about all this," she said.

"Whatever you want. Well, see you later!"

Together, Lillian and Josh moved ahead cautiously in the moonlight, and shortly afterward the friends waiting on the shore heard the creak of the metal joints as the oars were fitted into place.

"I can hardly wait until it's our turn," exclaimed Ricki excitedly. "Do you think we'll make it in fifteen minutes? Rowing out to the place where the bottle is and then back again?"

"You mean, you wonder if *I'll* make it, don't you?" Kevin laughed softly.

"Yes, but I didn't want to say it in so many words," she admitted, embarrassed.

"In that case, I'll prepare myself for a race."

"You guys are crazy! I'd –" Cathy broke off in the middle of her sentence. "Did you hear that?" she asked in a whisper.

"What?"

"That sneeze! I definitely heard a sneeze!"

"That was probably Josh or Lillian –"

"Nope, they're too far away! Anyway, it came from the right!"

Ricki and Kevin listened intently in every direction, and suddenly the heads of their horses shot upward.

"You're right, Cathy. There must be someone here!" whispered Ricki. "Stay calm, my darlings, no one's going to hurt you," she said quietly to the horses, who were snorting nervously, their nostrils flaring.

"Maybe we should go and investigate," whispered Kevin, but Cathy looked at him in fear, her eyes like saucers.

"I wouldn't dream of doing that. I hope that Josh and Lillian come back soon so that we can get out of here."

"But the bottle –"

"Forget the bottle!"

*

Unable to suppress his sneezing, the shivering man understood that it was only a matter of time before he would be discovered. And he couldn't let that happen.

There's only one thing to do – disappear myself, he thought, and he began, slowly and as quietly as possible, to wade through the water to where he could climb out onto the shore and run. He looked for his flashlight, but it was

82

nowhere to be found, so he had to orient himself by the light of the full moon.

*

"I think I could float here on the water with you forever," gushed Lillian, and let her hand drift in the cool water while Josh rowed forcefully. She watched the little ripple of water that flowed from her hand behind the boat.

"What a wonderful evening ... thousands of stars in the sky and this fantastic moon ... magical. Lily, how'd you like me to get you a star?" Josh pulled in the oars and put them lengthways into the boat, then he sat down next to Lillian, put an arm around her, and gave her a big squeeze.

"No, I don't want any of those stars. Let others enjoy them, too," responded the girl. Happy to be with her boyfriend, she enjoyed the slow drifting of the boat in the water.

After a minute, however, Josh returned to his seat and dipped the oars back into the water. "As much as I'd like to spend the whole evening here with you, I think we'd better get back. After all, Ricki and Kevin want to experience the magic, too. Anyway, the air out here is much colder than on shore, don't you think?"

Lillian nodded quietly.

A little chilly, she rubbed her arms and kept sniffing.

"OK, let's go back, before this cold that I've been nursing for about three weeks gets any worse. My English teacher complained that I was disrupting his class with all my nose blowing. Hey," she said suddenly and pointed behind the young man. "I didn't notice that we'd rowed out so far.

83

Look, there's that flashing that Ricki was talking about. Even the moonlight reflects on the bottle – that is, if it is a bottle."

Josh turned a little to the side and looked in the direction in which Lillian had pointed.

"You know what, since we're here anyway, let's row over there and get a closer look at that thing. Maybe it's nothing. Then Ricki and Kevin won't have to come out here."

The young man steered the boat to the exact location and was almost there after a few hefty strokes of the oars.

"Just a little more to the right," Lillian advised him. She was leaning far out over the boat. "A little more ... yeah, stop, that's perfect. I've almost got it!"

"It really is a bottle," she called out, amazed, and she tried to grab it, but it seemed to be anchored in place by an invisible power.

"There's a net around it," Lillian informed her boyfriend, who was trying hard to keep the boat straight and steady as Lillian leaned over the edge.

"Lily, stop, it's no use! We're going to capsize if you keep this up!"

"Wait, just a minute." Lillian reached for the stubborn object once more and screamed when her jerking movement caused the boat to tip over. They both landed in the water.

Blowing water out his mouth and nose, Josh appeared on the surface and looked around. "Lily, are you OK?" he asked as he coughed and tried to spit out the water he'd swallowed.

"I'm fine," the girl replied, and tried to swim to the overturned boat. But the combined weight of her riding boots and soaking-wet clothing made it difficult for her to make any progress. In addition, she felt a slight pain in her temples and in her right elbow, which had both hit the side of the boat when she fell in.

Josh swam the few yards toward the boat. When he reached it, he extended one hand to his girlfriend and held onto the boat with the other.

Gratefully, Lillian grabbed his hand and was glad when she finally felt the wood beneath her hands.

"What a mess, huh?" she asked, embarrassed, and looked sideways at Josh as they both clung to the overturned boat.

"Well, I've always wanted to go swimming at night with you," he said, grinning, although he wasn't really in the mood to make jokes.

"In riding clothes?"

"Of course! It wouldn't be as interesting in a bathing suit!"

"Yeah, well, to be honest, you probably wouldn't look as good in a bathing suit as you do in your Western duds!" she responded, relieved that Josh wasn't mad at her.

"We have to turn this thing around somehow! The only question is how we're going to do it. The boat's heavier than it looks!" he replied and looked very worried. "The best thing is for us to take a deep breath, then dive under a few feet, grab one side and try to push it upward."

Lillian nodded, and when Josh gave the signal, they both began their first attempt at getting the boat upright.

They didn't make it, and after the seventh attempt, Lillian panted, "That's it, I can't keep going anymore!"

Josh was running out of strength, too. "But somehow we've got to get back to the shore. Oh wait, I have an idea!"

He dove one more time and came up after a few seconds holding one of the oars.

"I was lucky. But I couldn't locate the other one," he panted, out of breath.

"What now?" asked Lillian.

"Now we're going to pull each other up on top of the boat and then try to get back by paddling!"

"You think that'll work?"

"I have no idea, but what choice do we have? Come on, I'll help you up!" Josh tried to pull Lillian up onto the keel of the boat, but she waved him off.

"Just a minute! If we fell in because of that stupid thing, then at least I want to know what it is," she said and then began to move along the boat, awkwardly, using her hands.

"You are really something," groaned Josh, a little annoyed. But Lillian had already stuck out her hand and pulled the mysterious bottle gently toward her.

"There must be something hanging down underneath," she said, breathing hard. "That's why it couldn't float to the shore! Josh, you have to help me!"

"I haven't been spared anything today," mumbled the young man as he grabbed the tough net that was woven around the bottle.

Lillian climbed up onto the keel of the boat with great effort. Then she took the bottle in one hand and held the oar tightly with the other.

"At least we're up here," Josh said as he climbed atop the boat. As he reached to take the bottle from Lillian, he said, "There's a thin rope tied to the bottle," and he began, little by little, to pull on the rope until a box, which was wrapped in layers of plastic to protect it from the water, appeared.

Josh and Lillian looked at each other bewildered.

"Lily, I have the feeling we've discovered something that will make somebody very upset," he said quietly.

"Ricki and her stubbornness!" fumed Lillian. "She was right again. But I really don't think there's a love letter hidden inside."

Josh nodded and gave the box and the bottle to his girlfriend. Then he grabbed the oar and paddled slowly forward, changing sides constantly as though he were paddling a canoe.

"It's going to take a while to get to shore," he said softly and was glad that the capsized boat was moving at all. "Maybe we should swim after all."

"But we can't just leave the boat out in the middle of the lake," said Lillian, as she was suddenly overwhelmed by a coughing fit.

"Hmm," responded Josh. "If we hold onto it and push it along, we could –"

"That's way too difficult! It'd take hours –" Before she finished her sentence, Lillian let out a scream. She'd leaned on her injured arm in order to turn toward Josh.

The young man was startled and scared. The last remaining oar slipped out of his hands and floated out of reach and sank immediately.

"Good grief, Lily! Why did you scream like that? What are we going to do now?" Josh's anger at his girlfriend was gone immediately when he realized that she was quietly sobbing.

"What's upsetting you? Tell me!"

Lillian cried quietly to herself while she held one hand over her injured elbow, which was throbbing horribly.

"It hurts so much," she stammered. "I hit my wrist a while ago, and now my whole arm is burning."

"Let me see." Josh bent over and touched her elbow gently. The girl groaned in pain. "Don't press on it," she pleaded.

"Now we really do have a problem," he said quietly before his glance went to the water's surface.

"I always thought that wood floats," whispered Lillian contritely.

"I thought so, too" agreed Josh. "Who knows why that stupid oar sank."

"How are we going to get back now?" asked the girl in a shaky voice.

"I have no idea."

*

"Hey, shouldn't those two have been back a long time ago? The quarter of an hour is up, don't you think? I hope nothing's happened to them," Cathy said, frightened.

"What could happen at night on Echo Lake?" asked Kevin. "They've probably forgotten all about the time, out there in their own little love boat," he said with a touch of sarcasm.

"I doubt anything has happened to them, but if they stay out much longer we won't be able to go rowing," Ricki commented, a little irritated, since she had to be home at nine o'clock sharp.

"The horses are getting nervous, too," complained Cathy. Ricki looked at her with annoyance. "Then why don't you just ride back home? Nothing makes you happy. You don't want to go boating, you don't want to wait, and you can't enjoy the night. Why did you come with us?"

"I already asked myself that! What are we going to do if –"

"Oh, come on, stop it. You're getting on my nerves!"

"But that sneeze –"

"Cathy, don't be a coward! I'm beginning to think we just imagined that sneeze, or else it really was Josh or Lily. Know what? I'm going to ride a few yards farther on so that I can see the water. It must be possible to see them in the moonlight." Ricki swung herself onto Diablo, who was glad that the ride was getting underway again.

"You can't go alone." Kevin, who was holding Sharazan and Doc Holliday's reins in his hand, was uneasy.

"Don't you start. I'll be right back!" Ricki urged her horse forward and rode him slowly across the strip of meadow and back onto the path around the lake.

Diablo's eyes, like Ricki's, had adjusted well to the darkness, and, with the help of the moonlight, neither had any trouble seeing the path in front of them.

"Well, my boy, at least now you'll have a little bit of exercise. Who would have thought that Josh and Lily would take such a long boat ride?" The girl spoke quietly to her horse, who trotted forward confidently.

After about thirty feet, Ricki stopped her horse. From here, she had a good view over most of Echo Lake, and she stared intently at the water, looking for the boat, but she could see nothing. "Where could they be?" she murmured to herself and rubbed her face nervously. Then she began to search the lake again, even more closely. Suddenly, she caught her breath. "Diablo, I must be dreaming! That ... that can't be. Come on, my good boy, we have to get back right away! It looks like those two out there need help."

Chapter 6

Richie and Jack stopped on the shore and stared in disbelief at the lake. The sound of excited young voices had caught their attention.

"Tell me this isn't happening," groaned Jack. "Those dumb kids are messing up our whole operation! What are we going to do now?"

Richie put his hands on his hips and kicked angrily at a root. "How should I know? I can only hope that all our work hasn't been for nothing!"

"Do you think we should –?"

"Quiet!" Richie grabbed his buddy by the shoulder. "Did you see that?"

Jack shook his head "What?" he asked quietly.

"Over there. Look, there's someone creeping through the underbrush!"

"It's probably one of those kids at the lake," said Jack, and he squinted his eyes until they began to water.

"No, I don't think so. The way he's darting from tree to tree, it's obvious that he doesn't want to be seen! You know what, though? I'm sick of all this. Langdon has no idea how difficult it is to bring the eggs in from the lake while people are strolling around here at all hours."

"And what's that?" asked Jack, pointing.

"A horse, what do you think it is? Don't tell me you've never seen a horse at night at Echo Lake."

"We should go over there and chase those guys away," said Jack angrily.

"And what would that accomplish? It would only make things worse. Anyway, I've got a feeling that this whole project is beginning to unravel. There's a different problem every night! Let's get out of here! Let Langdon find some other idiots to do his dirty work. Come on!"

*

I have to get out of here ... get away ... The man, breathing heavily, stumbled through the dark woods. *Now that those kids have found the bottle, the game is over ... everything's over. And it was all for nothing. What a pathetic loser I am. I should have known better, I should have known it couldn't work. What am I going to do now?*

*

"Hey, guys!" Ricki called to Kevin and Cathy as she rode toward them. "Lillian and Josh are in big trouble! They're sitting on the upturned boat in the middle of the lake, and they're just drifting!"

Kevin and Cathy, who jumped at the sound of Ricki's loud voice, were both thinking, *Ricki must be seeing things again! Upturned boat, indeed ... as if anyone could see anything from this distance.*

"Hey, Cathy, Kevin, are you guys still here? Can you hear me?" Ricki guided Diablo back to the green strip of meadow again. When she saw the large shadows of the waiting horses, and Sharazan greeted his stall mate Diablo with a happy whinny, the girl breathed a sigh of relief.

"Thanks a lot, you guys. Why didn't you answer me?" She was angry with her friends.

"We thought you might have fallen under the spell of the full moon and were having visions. Either that, or you were just playing one of your jokes on us. You know, Ricki, sometimes you –"

"For once, Kevin," she cut him off, "take me seriously! I wish it were only a joke, but it's not!" Ricki bit her lips. "Our friends are out there on the lake, stranded. They must have lost the oars. At least, I didn't see any."

"They can both swim, can't they?" asked Cathy, scared.

"Of course they can, but with their heavy riding boots and clothes on it won't be easy. I think we should all ride to a flat area, where we can observe the entire lake. And maybe we can figure out a way to help them. Let's ride over to the new campground. Then we'll see!"

Kevin sorted out the reins of the two horses that he was holding and then mounted Sharazan awkwardly. Ricki took Cherish from Cathy, so that her friend could mount as well, and together they left the place where only a short while before they had dreamed of a romantic adventure under a starry, moonlit sky.

There was nothing romantic about their situation, but it certainly was an adventure.

*

"Now we're really in trouble," said Josh, who snuggled up closer to Lillian and put his arm around her to warm her. She was soaking wet and shivering in the cool night air and her injured elbow throbbed with pain.

Lillian stared at the box she held tightly in both hands. "All because of this ... thing! I feel like throwing it back into the lake!" Freezing, she huddled against Josh who was trying to get his friends' attention by shouting, "Help!" loudly a few times in the direction of the shore.

"I hope somebody heard me."

"Anyone who didn't hear that is deaf," answered Lillian in a rough voice, her gaze still on the box. "But how can they help us?"

"I have faith in Ricki. She'll think of something. Maybe they'll be really smart and ride home to get an adult. What do you think, should I swim over there alone and –? No, bad idea!" he answered himself.

Lillian wasn't feeling well at all. In an effort to distract her, Josh said, "Come on, let's open that thing now! We don't have anything better to do!" Josh looked over Lillian's shoulder and observed how his girlfriend awk-wardly removed one layer of plastic after the other until a gray metal box appeared.

"This is worse than peeling onions," she joked when she finally held the cold metal in her hands. In spite of her awful situation, she regarded it with curiosity.

"Might as well forget it!" she said, disappointed. "The thing is locked."

"Give it to me!" Josh grabbed the box from Lillian and

examined it closely. "Oh, this is just an ordinary metal lock-box that you can buy at any hardware store! Wait a minute. If I still have my pocket knife, the lock is as good as open!"

Josh rummaged around in his pockets and then Lillian heard the sound of the knife working on the lock.

"Got it?" she asked, but she didn't dare turn around for fear that any movement would send them into the water again.

"Wait! I'll have it in a minute. Yeah! Got it! Now let's see, what the –" Josh was shocked into silence when he saw the contents of the box.

"And? What is it?" asked Lillian impatiently. "Love letter or treasure map? Tell me."

"Neither nor," Josh answered, and held a bundle of money under Lillian's nose.

"What ... what is that?" she asked.

"That is a lot of cash someone has hidden in the lake for a rainy day! My guess is it's the loot from the recent burglaries," announced Josh, who put the money back into the box and clapped the lid shut.

"Anything else?"

"That's enough!"

*

Ricki, Cathy, and Kevin arrived at the new campground, which was only used a few months in the year so as not to disturb the breeding habits of the ducks.

"Now we should be able to see a little more clearly," said Ricki quietly. With her heart beating wildly, she jumped down from Diablo's back.

The friends could now recognize Josh and Lillian fairly easily. They were sitting completely motionless on top of the boat. Suddenly, Josh's scream for help shrilled through the night.

"Help! ... Can anybody hear me? Help!"

"Hey, helloooo ... we're over here!" Ricki shouted in response. She jumped up and down and waved her arms wildly.

Lillian looked up. "Did you hear that?" she asked excitedly.

Josh nodded. "Yeah! Sounds like Ricki, I'd say. But I couldn't make out what she said!"

The couple gazed all around searching for them, and finally Josh spotted the group of riders on the shore. "Look, Lillian, they're over there." He raised his arms and waved to signal his friends that he'd seen them.

"Oops!" he said, and grabbed quickly for the metal box, which had started to slide as he was waving his arms around. "That was close! The thing almost got away!"

"That's all we need! Then all of this would really have been for nothing." Lillian was exasperated.

"I've just about had enough of this," grumbled Josh, upset. "We've got to find a way to get back to the shore!" He frowned and tried to concentrate. "You're in no shape to swim," he said to his shivering girlfriend.

"No, I'm not. I'm freezing to death," groaned Lillian at her boyfriend's suggestion. "Maybe you should go alone. I'll stay here and I won't move. I'll hold the box!"

"Absolutely not an option," said Josh, determined. "I'm not going to leave you or the box or the boat! Who knows? The guys who hid this money might come back for it. If, as I think, this is the loot from the burglaries, then the boat is evidence for the police. The thieves know that, and there's no telling what they might do to you to cover up their crime."

Lillian tried to control her chattering teeth and was silent.

"I think the only thing I can do is take off my boots and jeans, get into the water, and push you and the boat to the shore. By the time Ricki and company make a decision about what to do, we'll be frozen to death," sighed Josh, but Lillian shook her head firmly.

"By the time we got to the shore, you'd be frozen anyway. I already am, and I have a headache, too. I bumped my head when we were trying to get the boat turned over."

"What? I thought it was your elbow."

"That, too!"

"Darn! Is it bad?" asked Josh, worried.

"It's not too bad, but I am a little dizzy," Lillian answered, trembling with the cold. She didn't want to alarm Josh, but her head felt like it was about to burst.

Josh glanced at the illuminated dial on his watch. "Oh-oh, it's eight thirty. Ricki's going to be in a lot trouble with her mother," he commented, staring at the box full of money that lay in his lap. *Who filled it?* he wondered. *Who hid it out here in the lake?*

*

While Cathy whined quietly and Kevin stared silently at the lake, Ricki was busy thinking.

Would it be possible … with Diablo? Pensively she looked at her horse. *No*, she thought, and let her gaze wander.

"The lasso! I think Josh brought his lasso with him!" she said, her face brightening.

96

"Do you want to lasso the boat? Come on, Ricki, that's no good!" Kevin tapped his forehead.

"Why not? I have an idea, but I'm not sure that Diablo will play along. Cherish would be more likely to, but Diablo is stronger. If I took ... Oh God, tell me what to do ..." Ricki was rambling, and Cathy and Kevin just looked at each other knowingly.

"Yeah, I'll try it!" Ricki passed Diablo's and Cherish's reins to Cathy, who didn't have a clue as to what she was planning, and began to unsaddle Diablo.

"Ahem, Ricki, would you please explain to us what you're doing?" asked Kevin, who also had absolutely no idea what was going on.

"Just a minute!" Quickly she walked around Cherish, unbuckled the saddlebags, and threw them on the ground. Then she unbuckled the saddle as well, and carried it over to Diablo, where she swung it onto his back.

"Hey, what's that supposed to be? Are you planning to do some Western training with Diablo?"

"Sorta!" Ricki tightened the saddle girth.

"Are you crazy!" burst out of Kevin, but Ricki just ignored him.

Quickly she took her horse's reins and walked him a few yards back and forth before she tightened the girth again.

Ricki wanted to tell her two friends what she was planning, but she knew that they would try to talk her out of it, and she wanted to avoid that at all costs. So she decided she wouldn't say anything to them until she was ready and mounted on Diablo.

"Hey, are you out of your mind? What are you doing? Ricki, what's going on? Talk to me!" Kevin looked at his girlfriend in bewilderment, and Cathy's face was getting paler by the minute.

Ricki paid no attention to them and struggled to take off her riding boots and socks. Finally barefoot, she lifted herself into the Western saddle.

"Yes!" she said with a sense of satisfaction. "Now we can start!"

Kevin had finally figured out what she was planning. "You're not serious, are you? You don't really want to do this, do you?" he asked, unsure whether he should be angry with his girlfriend for her foolhardiness or admire her for her courage.

Ricki nodded. "Yes, I do! And before you two say anything, just listen!" Gravely she looked into the two baffled faces.

"This is what I'm going to try to do – Diablo will swim out to the boat with me on his back. Then I'll attach the lasso to him and the boat and Diablo will tow it back to shore. That's why I'm using the Western saddle. I can tie the lasso to the pommel."

"You're totally crazy. What if –?"

"I said listen!" Ricki interrupted her girlfriend firmly. "In the meantime, Cathy, you take care of Holli, Cherish, and Rashid, while Kevin rides home as fast as possible." Ricki stared at her boyfriend.

"Tell my parents anything you have to, but make sure that one of them comes here with the car and a bundle of warm blankets. I think the three of us will be freezing by the time Mom or Dad gets here. Oh, yeah, and bring a horse blanket for Diablo. He'll be as wet as we are! OK? Here goes!"

"Ricki, stay here. This is crazy! The two of them can

swim in by themselves, can't they?" Kevin felt the fear for his girlfriend growing inside him.

"There must be a reason why they haven't done that," replied Ricki. "Anyway, even though they're pretty far out, Diablo can make it. I can hold on to him. There's no better swimming aid than a horse!"

"Please, Ricki, get down right now and let me go!" pleaded Kevin. He looked to Cathy for assistance, but she just shrugged her shoulders anxiously.

"See ya," Ricki said, ignoring Kevin's pleas and turning Diablo toward the water. "And don't forget to bring the blankets!"

"Ricki, NO!" screamed Kevin, but Ricki just said, "OK, Diablo, let's go for a swim," and she urged him forward. "I know we can do it."

*

"Marcus!" Brigitte pushed open the living room door and stared at her husband, who was relaxing on the couch, watching TV.

"What's up?" he asked sleepily.

"Ricki and the others aren't back yet!" Brigitte's sounded extremely worried. "She promised me that she'd be back by nine o'clock, and it's almost ten minutes past."

Ricki's father just smiled. "They're probably just enjoying their ride up to the last second, Brigitte. I'm sure they'll be back any minute now. After all, there are five of them, and there's safety in numbers."

"Marcus, I'm really worried," Brigitte's voice trembled. "Couldn't we drive along the path?"

Marcus sat up. Brigitte had managed to infect him with her concern.

"We'll give them another fifteen minutes. If they haven't turned up by then, I'll get in the car and go looking for them. Don't worry. I'm sure they were having so much fun they just forgot all about the time."

"If only I hadn't let myself be talked into this," whispered Ricki's mother, and she focused her attention on the hands of the clock.

*

Kevin had handed over Holli's reins to Cathy with shaking hands. White as a sheet, she stared after Ricki and Diablo, incapable of saying anything.

The boy wanted to jump up onto his horse, but just as he put his foot in the stirrup, the saddle fell off sideways.

"That's all I need!" In the excitement, Kevin had forgotten to tighten the girth, and now he had to reposition the saddle. His hands didn't seem to want to obey him. Awkwardly he tugged at the saddle blanket. After what seemed like an eternity, he was able to mount.

"Cathy, hang tough. I'll be back as quickly as possible!"

Cathy nodded silently and watched him until he and Sharazan disappeared into the darkness of the woods.

*

After the first few hesitant steps in the water, Diablo was surprised that Ricki didn't lead him back to shore like she usually did.

100

He stood still for a few seconds, snorted happily, and beat his front hooves on the surface of the water.

"Don't even think about getting down and rolling," Ricki warned her horse, and just to make sure she shortened the reins. "We don't have time for any nonsense now!" She urged him onward, firmly, and with each step the black horse went deeper and deeper into the water. Before long, Ricki realized that he was no longer walking on the sandy lake bottom but was swimming strongly forward.

"You are wonderful, my good boy, the best horse in the world. Keep going, you're doing really well," she whispered to him tenderly. Gently she dismounted and carefully positioned herself next to him, holding onto the pommel of the saddle with one hand.

Ricki had completely loosened the reins and used them only to guide him in the right direction. *I hope this works*, she kept thinking. *We've gone too far to turn back.*

*

Kevin had his flashlight with him, but he didn't need it for the ride home. The light from the full moon was so bright that he had no trouble recognizing the road. The boy would need the flashlight only to alert any oncoming car of his presence.

Sharazan knew the way by heart. The kids had ridden along here countless times with their horses.

Kevin himself knew that there were no obstacles along the way and therefore he could risk galloping without worrying that his horse could misstep and injure his leg.

"Come on, come on, boy, I know that galloping at night

isn't what you're used to, but we've got to get home. I just hope Ricki's mother doesn't bite my head off."

Sharazan fell into a fast trot by himself, finding that pace a little safer. The animal and his rider were making good progress. They would be out of the woods soon, and at this pace they would reach their destination in about ten minutes.

But Kevin was terribly afraid for his girlfriend.

Why does she have to be so stubborn? Why does she always have to have her own way? he asked himself.

He was just beginning to recognize the familiar lights of the Sulai farm in the distance when, from out of nowhere, a car appeared behind them. It sped past them and down the country road.

Kevin hadn't heard it coming and thought it was because of his preoccupation with Ricki. Nevertheless, he stared incredulously after the beat-up red vehicle illuminated by the moon. Driving at that speed on these little roads was simply irresponsible!

Kevin fixed his eyes on the car's license plate as it sped away. He had a feeling that this number would be important later.

*

"All of a sudden I feel sick to my stomach," groaned Lillian, and she pressed her hands to her head. When she looked up at the sky, the stars began to turn and twist before her eyes. "I think I'm going to fall over!"

"Don't you dare, Lillian Bates!" Josh pulled her closer to him. *If only I knew how to get us ashore*, he tortured himself. Suddenly he yelled to his friends on land.

102

"Hey, Hel-looo! Can you hear me? Lillian's sick! You've got to go and get help for us. We can't make it back to shore by ourselves. Do you hear me? We're stranded," he shouted. Then to Lillian he murmured, "Don't be afraid. They'll find a way get us back on land," and stroked her hair lovingly.

"Ouch!" Lillian made a face, and Josh jerked back instinctively.

"What's the matter?" he asked softly, but when the girl didn't answer, he bent down over her head and discovered dried blood, which had soaked her hair.

"You really banged your head bad, Lilly. Why didn't you tell me right away?

"I'm soooo nauseated," she kept repeating quietly and reached out with her hand for Josh. "Are we at the shore yet?"

Josh took a deep breath. "No, sweetheart, not yet. But it won't be much longer," he lied. He'd never felt so helpless in his life.

*

"Marcus, I can't stand this waiting any longer! Please, do something! I'm really afraid that something bad has happened!" Brigitte paced back and forth in the room like a caged tiger.

"All right!" Ricki's father got up and grabbed his car keys. "You stay here! After all, we can't leave Harry alone!"

Reluctantly Brigitte nodded and accompanied her husband to the front door.

"Don't worry, the kids will be here sooner than you th–"

"Mrs. Sulai, Mr. Sulai, helloooo," Kevin's voice echoed loudly across the yard and interrupted Marcus's words.

"See, what did I tell you?" Marcus smiled at his wife before he opened the door.

"Well, Kevin, are all your watches slow?" he called out genially. But when he saw that the boy was alone he became silent and anxious.

"Please, quick, come with me to the lake. We need blankets for the kids and a horse blanket for Diablo. Josh and Lillian are stranded in the middle of the lake on an overturned boat, and Ricki and Diablo have swum out to try to pull them in. I'll come with you!" Kevin's voice broke as he sprang out of Sharazan's saddle.

"What are you yelling about, Kevin?" Jake called from his window, but when he saw only Sharazan in the yard, he hurried outside.

"What are you saying?" asked Marcus. "Ricki and Diablo are swimming in the lake?" Marcus repeated Kevin's words in disbelief, and he needed a moment to calm down.

"We should go. The blankets –" Kevin looked around desperately.

Jake grabbed Sharazan's reins. "Go, get the blankets!" he instructed the boy, who gazed at Brigitte questioningly.

Ricki's mother ran back to the house stiffly, like a robot, and came back with several thick plaid blankets while Kevin ran into the stable and grabbed Diablo's horse blanket.

"I knew something like this would happen!" murmured Brigitte as though in shock. "But I never thought she'd be foolish enough to swim in Echo Lake at night with her horse. Marcus, your daughter must be crazy!"

104

Ricki's father took the blankets from her. "Kevin, come with me! You can tell me all about it on the way! Brigitte, I –"

Ricki's mother just sighed in exasperation. "Get going!" she said quietly, and then she turned to Jake. She whispered, "I don't think I'll ever get over all the excitement Ricki and Diablo have caused. It seems that every other week they're getting into trouble. And, Jake, in the future please don't try to get me to change my mind about anything concerning Ricki. Do you understand me?"

The old man nodded and led Sharazan into the stable. He was stung by Brigitte's rebuke.

It was true that Ricki and Diablo had gotten into some scrapes, and he understood Brigitte's concern, but he wished she would also realize how well, for the most part, Ricki had handled herself in these situations. *The kids are growing up*, he thought. *And they're doing a fine job of it, if you ask me.* But that didn't make him any less worried.

Chapter 7

The speeding car careened dangerously along the narrow curves of the country road. The driver stared dully out of the windshield, the steering wheel gripped by his sweating hands. He had a lot on his mind.

He kept steady pressure on the gas pedal and, as if in a trance, raced his vehicle through the moonlit night. After many winding miles, finally overcome with exhaustion, the driver slowed his car and turned off the road. *I've got to sleep*, he said to himself. He shut off the engine and let his head sink down into his hands. But the memory of recent events – and his sense of failure – would give him no peace.

Everything that could go wrong had gone wrong. There was nothing left to salvage. All the work – all the risk – had been for nothing. Life seemed senseless to him. He could no longer find any reason to hope. The last bit of strength had been drained from him and he was unashamed as tears ran down his stubbly cheeks.

"I've failed – failed – failed!" he shouted into the empty darkness. Rest was going to be impossible. He pulled himself together, turned the engine back on, eased the car back onto the road, and continued his drive home ... a home that would never be the same, because he would soon be reminded of his failure every day.

*

Relentlessly, Diablo pushed his way through the water, bringing Ricki closer and closer to the capsized boat. The girl's legs were beginning to get stiff from the coldness of the water, and she began to worry that the cold water might take a toll on Diablo's legs as well.

She toyed briefly with the idea of turning back, but when she heard Josh's desperate cries, she knew retreat was not an option.

"Diablo," she said with a confidence she did not feel, "we can't turn back. Do you have any strength left? Our friends need us."

"Help us, please. Lillian's sick!" Josh's voice was beginning to sound desperate.

"We're coming," Ricki called back. "What's wrong with Lillian?"

The young man on the boat shivered. How could this be? Had he just heard Ricki's voice, and so near? Then why couldn't he see her?

"Ricki? Where are you?" he called loudly, but before she could answer, he spotted Diablo's dark head in the water and, swimming along side, Ricki. The young man's heart nearly burst with relief.

"I can't believe it," he said quietly to himself. "I ... I must be hallucinating. Ricki and her horse here, in the middle of the lake? She must be crazy. But I'm so glad to see her."

"Diablo is going to tow you to shore," Ricki called to him. She hoped that Diablo had enough strength left to pull this maneuver off.

"You're crazy," yelled Josh. "He'll never make it! He's not used to swimming that far, especially pulling a weight!"

She hadn't come this far to be told that she and Diablo couldn't make it. That would have to be proven. "I brought your lasso," she pressed on. "I've tied one end to the pommel of your saddle, which I put on Diablo. Now all we have to do is tie the other end to the boat somehow."

Josh went pale. *She's serious*, he thought. Then he realized what Ricki had just said.

"You put my Western saddle on Diablo? What were you thinking? In the first place, it's thirty pounds of extra weight for the animal, and secondly –"

"Oh, stop arguing with me," screamed Ricki, furious. It seemed like everyone was telling her what she could and couldn't do. "Do you think Diablo and I are out here to enjoy a midnight swim? This was the best plan I could come up with to help you guys. Now, stop quibbling and take the end of the lasso and tie it to the boat somewhere, somehow," she commanded, and then, in a softer voice, she added, "unless can you think of a way we can get Lillian to shore without using the boat? That would be much easier," panted Ricki, as she and Diablo treaded water.

"Maybe we could lie her across Diablo's back, but then we'd have to swim right next to him to keep her from falling off," suggested Josh.

But Ricki knew there wasn't much time to think about it. Soon Diablo's strength would begin to ebb. Abruptly, she let go of her horse and swam over to the boat, holding her

108

end of the lasso. Josh put the box down next to Lillian and slid into the water beside Ricki.

"Where can we tie this?" she asked. Without answering, he took the rope from her. He would tie it to the giant metal ring that was used to moor the boat.

"Keep Diablo calm," he called to her and dove under the boat to find the ring.

Groaning, Lillian moved on the top of the boat.

"Lily, is everything OK?" From her position in the water, Ricki couldn't see much of her girlfriend.

"Ricki, I'm so glad you're here," she answered feebly.

"Lily ... Lillian, can you hold on to the box?" Josh asked as he surfaced after securing the lasso to the mooring ring. "I'm going to help Ricki and Diablo pull the boat to the shore, OK?"

Lillian reached for the metal box and held it tightly in both hands. She didn't even notice that the boat had slowly begun to move. She was confused. *Diablo? Josh said something about Diablo. What's that horse doing out here?*

*

The waiting was driving Cathy crazy with anxiety, so it was a great relief when she saw Mr. Sulai's car drive onto the campground with Kevin in the passenger seat.

"Where are they?" Kevin asked as he jumped from the still-moving car and rushed over to Cathy. "Please don't tell me they're still out there." Horrified, Kevin stared out at Echo Lake. "I can't see them anymore!" he called out in panic and ran into the water up to his hips.

"Kevin, come back here immediately!" Marcus's voice thundered over the campground. "Immediately!"

Ricki's boyfriend jumped.

"But, but they're gone! That ... that just can't be. Where are they? They haven't –"

Cathy's eyes filled with tears. She thought the pressure she felt in her throat was going to suffocate her.

Ricki's father grabbed Kevin's arm and pulled him out of the water. The three stood silently on the shore and stared out across the shimmering surface. It should have been a peaceful, tranquil moment, and at any other time it would have been. But now, all they could think about was the fate of Ricki, Josh, and Lillian. And Diablo, of course.

*

It was late. Dr. Kennedy lay on the couch in his hospital office staring at the ceiling. He was dead tired, but he couldn't sleep.

The abrupt ringing of his telephone jolted him from his reverie. He certainly hadn't been expecting any calls this late at night.

A glance at the blinking button told him that it wasn't an inner-hospital call. "An outside call, at this time of night? Who can it be?" He went to his desk, picked up the receiver, and answered with a little irritation.

"Dr. Kennedy here."

"Hello, Phil. Working the night shift, are you?"

"Tom! I didn't expect a call from you at this hour." Dr. Kennedy leaned back in his large chair.

"I thought I'd take a chance. I think you won't mind the

interruption when I tell you what I've been able to work out. It's about your spine case. I've looked through my lecture schedule, and I see that Pittsburgh comes up next month. I called the University Hospital today, and I was able to schedule the date a little sooner. That means that you can pick me up at the airport day after tomorrow. I'll let you know the exact time of arrival."

"I knew you wouldn't let me down, Tom!"

"But I'll have only three days for you, and then I have to go back to Boston. That means we'll have to work overtime."

"And what does that mean, exactly?" Dr. Kennedy took the cordless phone into the central file room next to his office.

"It means that on the first day I'll do a complete examination of the young lady, with the exception of blood tests, which you should have finished by the time I arrive. In addition, I'd like to have new X-rays and a CAT scan of the complete spine, and also an MRI."

"At least you're not too demanding!" laughed Dr. Kennedy as he searched for Lissy Benson's file in the patients' file cabinet labeled A – C.

"In the evening, after I've had a chance to review the data," continued Dr. Albright, "we'll put our heads together and decide whether or not it makes sense to operate on the young lady. If it's a go, we'll schedule the operation for the next day. Prepare yourself and your surgical team for a very long and difficult operation. I'd estimate a minimum of six hours. I'm sure you'll have everything ready for me."

Dr. Kennedy grinned. "You can count on it!"

"OK, Phillip. That's all for now. I'm glad I was able to

work this out. It'll be good to work with you again. So long. You'll be hearing from me."

"Bye, Tom ... and ... thanks."

"Bye, Phil!"

Dr. Kennedy hung up the phone, clamped Lissy's file under his arm, and went back to his office. First thing tomorrow morning he would order new blood tests for the young woman and examine her vital signs to see if she would be able to undergo such a risky operation. There shouldn't be any complications, but he didn't want to take any chances.

Dr. Kennedy would have loved to go straight to Lissy Benson and tell her that his colleague, Dr. Thomas Albright, an eminent specialist in neurosurgery, had taken an interest in her case. But he knew that it was better to raise no hope than to offer false hope. Nevertheless, he decided to look in on the young woman. He attached his beeper to his belt and left his office.

He walked briskly down the long, quiet corridor, past the nurses' station, where the night shift nurse was just making fresh coffee, and carefully opened the door, behind which lay Lissy Benson in her body cast.

The light on the emergency button was on, and it gave Lissy's face a strange, orange glow.

Dr. Kennedy sat down for a moment on a chair beside the hospital bed and regarded the sleeping young woman thoughtfully.

"Sleep well, Lissy, and dream about something good." Unnoticed, he slipped out again and stopped at the nurses' station on his way back to his office.

"Do you happen to have another cup of strong coffee for a totally exhausted werewolf?" he asked grinning.

The night nurse laughed.

"Ah, another full-moon victim! Well, then, come on in, Doctor. My coffee has cured every werewolf syndrome there is!"

*

Ricki could see that Diablo was beginning to tire. His legs didn't move as powerfully and rhythmically through the water as they had on the way out to the boat, and it looked as though he was settling a lot deeper in the water than before.

The sudden weight of the boat had confused Diablo and made him whinny angrily, and that had caused him to get water in his nose, which had frightened him and made him unsure of himself. Only after a lot of loving and tender encouragement from Ricki did he calm down, but he still kept looking back at the boat with a frightened expression in his eyes. It kept following him.

Ricki tried to estimate the distance to the shore. *Oh, no*, she thought, with a frightened look at her horse. *I overestimated him! Diablo will never make it! Never! I'm such an idiot!*

"Hey, Ricki, guide Diablo sharply to the left, do you hear me? Left!" Josh waved his arm wildly behind the boat.

"Why?"

"Don't ask questions! Just do it!"

"Come on, my boy. Josh says left, so we'll go left!" Gently, she pulled on the appropriate rein a little. But the horse came out of his disrupted rhythm and began to kick wildly, making him even unsteadier.

113

"Diablo, calm down. Easy, boy. Please, don't give up! Please, keep going. It can't be much farther," she pleaded with her horse, but she was hardly able to move herself. The cold water seemed to have paralyzed her muscles. Her nerves were completely shattered and physically she was a wreck.

"Terrific! Good job," Josh called to her. "That's exactly the right direction! Ricki, if I'm correct, we'll be there very soon! Still about three hundred feet, and then Diablo should sense ground under his hooves. Can you hear me, Ricki?"

The girl heard Josh's voice, but she was no longer able to answer him. *A hundred yards*, she thought. *If he's not mistaken! And what if he is mistaken?*

A twitch went through Diablo's body. He seemed to sense that he would soon be relieved of this terrible burden, and he used all of his reserves to reach the shore as quickly as possible.

Ricki felt like a marionette. All she could do was move her arms and legs mechanically. She had no feeling in them anymore.

"I can't keep going," called Ricki to Josh quietly.

"Ricki Sulai, you can do it! You can't give up now with only a few yards to go! You'll make it! Understand? No, *we'll* make it! Do you hear me?"

Ricki nodded. *Yeah, yeah*, she thought wearily. *We'll make it! But I'm so exhausted ... so terribly exhausted ... so ...*

Diablo whinnied loudly and didn't seem to be moving.

"Good heavens, Diablo, swim. You can't stop now ... you ..."

Ricki screamed hysterically at her horse, but Diablo just turned his head toward her and looked at her with his wise eyes.

Don't get so excited, he seemed to say before he started moving again, and slowly and carefully put his hooves down on the muddy lake bottom and walked toward the shore.

Ricki needed a moment to comprehend that they had, in fact, made it, that they had done something superhuman this evening.

"I can't believe it," she whispered, trembling with exhaustion, excitement, and cold. "Diablo, thank you, thank you. You are ... you are simply the most fabulous creature on this planet!" The girl laughed and cried at the same time when she finally felt the ground beneath her feet, and with her last ounce of strength she fought her way through the final yards of water. Then she just let herself collapse on the shore next to Diablo, who had come to a halt when the boat had started dragging on the lake bottom and remained there motionless.

Josh held his breath and hoped that Ricki's horse would stay standing calmly, while he carefully took Lillian in his arms and carried her with shaky steps to land. He set her down carefully. She was still holding the box tightly in both her hands.

As quickly as he could, he ran over to Diablo and cut through the girth of his Western saddle with his pocketknife. He couldn't see any other way to free the horse from his burden. The knot of the soaking-wet leather girth was impossible to undo by hand,

"You are a really, really good boy, Diablo," whispered Josh quietly to the trembling horse. "I'll never forget what you did tonight. Never!" And he gave Diablo a big kiss on his throbbing muzzle.

Ricki struggled to get up and grabbed Diablo's reins, shivering.

"Is Lillian OK?" she asked hoarsely, and Josh nodded.

"I think so. But I have no idea how we're going to get her home," he said, worried. He knelt down next to his girlfriend.

"Lillian, can you hear me?" he asked and stroked her face tenderly.

The girl nodded weakly. "Are we home yet?" she asked softly.

Josh squeezed her hand. "Not quite yet, but at least we're on dry land. Ricki and Diablo pulled us ashore. Aren't they great?"

"Hmm," said Lillian before she sank back into semi-consciousness.

Ricki was totally exhausted. The idea of going even one yard farther seemed impossible, but considering her shivering horse, she made herself get up and hobble slowly back and forth with him. She didn't even notice that she wasn't wearing any shoes. The cold water had made her feet completely numb.

Josh got up awkwardly and stared across to the other side of the lake. "We have to try to get someone's attention," he mumbled. Then he took a deep breath. "Hellooooo ... we're here ... we're on land. Hellooooo, Cathy, Kevin!" he yelled, as loudly as he could. He formed a funnel with his hands around his mouth, and shouted even louder, and then he let his hands fall to his sides, completely worn out.

"Do you have the flashlight that you found in the boat?" asked Ricki, with a scratchy voice.

Josh hesitated a moment, and then he understood.

Excitedly, he patted down all of his pockets and then brought out the flashlight, still intact.

"That's one thing tight jeans are good for," he said and tried to smile. "Nothing falls out. Let's just hope that the water didn't ruin it! Ricki, keep your fingers crossed!"

The girl nodded and then stared at the little flashlight, which went on after only three tries.

The two young people sighed with relief and hoped that their friends would notice the blinking light, which they shone over the lake.

"By the way, I sent Kevin to let my parents know what happened," Ricki suddenly remembered. Josh gave her a hug and kissed her gratefully on the cheek.

"You're really something, you know that? A girl in a million! Thank you so much!" he said, and then he went back to Lillian.

Ricki tortured herself by walking up and down with Diablo so that his circulation would slowly return to normal after all this hard work.

*

Kevin and Ricki's father hugged each other in relief, and Cathy gave a shout as they heard Josh's voice echoing across the lake. They were able to see the tiny beam of light from the flashlight, which showed them the exact location of the stranded teenagers.

"Can we drive there with the car?" asked Marcus excitedly, and Kevin nodded.

"Keep on the circular road, and it'll take you right there!" explained Kevin."

117

"Good!" Ricki's father sprang into his car immediately and started the engine. "You guys ride straight home!"

Kevin shook his head. Quickly he threw Ricki's boots, her socks, and Josh's saddlebags through the window onto the back seat.

"No, I think we'll ride over there, too. After all, Diablo has to get back to the stable, and I doubt that Ricki is still capable of riding him."

Marcus wrinkled his forehead.

"OK! But hurry!" he called to them, and then he drove off with screeching tires.

Quickly Kevin saddled Cherish, while Cathy held on to her reins.

"Diablo's saddle is almost too big for her," realized Kevin, distracted.

Cathy knew that Kevin was very worried about his girlfriend. "She's ... she's fine. Ricki's OK, you'll see," she said softly and put her hand on the boy's shoulder.

Kevin nodded and tried to hold back his tears of relief. "Come on," he said quietly, "we have to get going!"

*

Ricki and Josh could hear the sound of a car's engine. "That's Dad!" shouted Ricki.

"Man, I'm so glad this nightmare is over." Quickly Josh ran up the slope to signal where they were so Ricki's father wouldn't drive past them.

"What kind of mess did you guys get yourselves into this time?" scolded Marcus as he got out of the car, but there was relief in his voice. "Is everyone OK?"

118

Josh shook his head.

"More or less, Mr. Sulai! Thanks for coming! Lillian is lying down there on the shore. She hit her head and now she's sick to her stomach. I don't know exactly what's wrong with her. She's so quiet ..."

Marcus ran off and slid down the slope. He reached Ricki and wrapped his arms around her in a big hug.

"Are you OK? You and Diablo?" he asked hastily as his glance fell on Lillian.

Ricki nodded. "But Lillian –"

"I know. I think the best thing is for me to take her to the hospital right away. She's obviously cold and she's barely conscious." Marcus looked back and forth between his shivering daughter and Josh. "And you two! Look at you! You're freezing! Come with me!"

Ricki's father picked up Lillian and carried her to the car. He placed her on the back seat and wrapped her in two blankets, after throwing one each to Ricki and Josh.

"Wrap them around your shoulders," he ordered, but Ricki shook her head.

"First Diablo," she shivered, and she could hardly keep her hands still as she reached for the horse blanket.

"Wrap yourself up in that darn blanket, daughter – now! I'll take care of Diablo!" Marcus looked at her so sternly she knew he would not allow any argument.

"As soon as Kevin and Cathy get here, we'll leave! You have to get out of those wet clothes and into a hot bath," Ricki's father decided. He watched, bewildered, as Josh ran back down the slope to the shore.

"Where's he going?" he asked, but before anyone could answer, Josh reappeared carrying his dripping wet saddle over his arm. In his right hand he held the mysterious metal money box, which had caused the whole mess.

Marcus opened the trunk and put Josh's saddle inside. Then he noticed the metal box, and without asking, threw it in, too. When the box hit the trunk it sprang open and wads of cash came bursting out of it. Marcus looked at Josh, flabbergasted.

"What's that?" he asked. Trembling with the cold, Ricki looked at the money, which was now spread all over the trunk of the car.

"You went out to the bottle?" she asked quietly, and Josh nodded.

"So it wasn't a love letter after all!" Ricki tried to laugh, but she couldn't quite manage it.

"I think the money is from the recent burglaries," Josh explained.

Marcus looked at him seriously before he shut the trunk. "First I'm going to call your mother, who is probably worried to death, and then I'll inform the police. If it's what you say, Josh, then ... Well, let's wait and see."

Marcus got out his cell phone as Josh got in the back seat beside Lillian and laid her head in his lap.

"You'll be fine," he whispered and stroked her hands.

I hope Kevin and Cathy come soon. Diablo has to get back to the stable. I don't want him to get sick after all this, thought Ricki, worried, but she dismissed the notion that she herself stood a good chance of catching pneumonia.

Chapter 8

It was late Sunday afternoon and, although the weather was beautiful, Ricki was in her room, wrapped in a heavy sweater. Her eyes were watering and she had a runny nose. Unlike yesterday, when her health seemed fine, the aftereffects of her late-night life-saving adventure were noticeable today.

Kevin opened the door, balancing a large mug of hot lemon tea and a plate of sugar cookies on a tray. It was touching how he was taking care of his girlfriend, who felt miserable with her cold, especially since she'd much prefer to be outside on these warm late-summer days.

"Greetings from your mother," he told her, grinning. "She said you have to drink the tea while it's still hot, so that the lemons won't lose their effect."

Ricki made a disgusted face. "I hate lemon tea!" she said with emphasis and sniffed loudly. "Has Mom calmed down yet? She was still furious this morning."

"Oh, no, she's not furious. She's just thankful that nothing happened to you. But, just between us, she can't admit it," whispered Kevin, glancing at the door to make sure it was closed and that Mrs. Sulai couldn't hear him. "Your mother squeezed at least six lemons for this tea. If you drink it, you'll probably become as sour as a lemon yourself."

"I am anyway," Ricki said, in a terrible mood. "Just look outside. It's Sunday, bright with sunshine, and I'm inside and too worn out to do anything. You'll see, tomorrow, when there's school, I'll be totally fine again."

"Yeah, yeah, Ricki, life is cruel!" Kevin looked at her sympathetically.

"Have you heard anything about Lillian?" she asked.

The boy nodded. "Josh called this morning and said that she's doing relatively well. She has a bad bruise on her head, a sprained elbow, and an upper respiratory infection. But the doctor says she'll be fine and is letting her go home today. She has to take antibiotics and stay in bed for a few days, the doctor said." Kevin thought it over. "It's possible that she's already home. The only one who apparently didn't have any ill effects from the whole thing is Josh. He's fine, like always!"

Ricki nodded. "And so is Diablo. Apart from sore muscles, he's fine, thank goodness!"

"They're guys," grinned Kevin, but Ricki just shook her head. She wasn't in the mood for any fake macho stuff.

Kevin sat down next to Ricki and put his arm around her.

"Hey, I'm so proud of you!" he said softly, which drew a smile from Ricki. "Even though you're not a guy –"

"You just can't leave it alone, can you?"

Kevin shook his head. "No! Otherwise I'd have to admit that, unlike you, I'm a coward! I don't think I'd have dared to swim out on the lake with Sharazan or Diablo, and certainly not to drag a tipped-over boat to shore with my horse."

122

Ricki turned bright red. "I wouldn't do it again, either," she said softly, and thought about how scared she had been for Diablo.

For a long time the two of them sat there and silently reflected on the night on Echo Lake. It would take a while for the memories to fade – if they ever did.

They were so deep in their thoughts that they were startled when they heard a knock on Ricki's door.

"Am I disturbing you?" Marcus asked, as he came into the room. "The police just called. They're sending someone to ask you some questions about the money box. By the way, since they determined that the money you kids found was indeed from the burglaries, they've decided not to press charges for the illegal boating," he said and pointed to the mug of tea. "You're supposed to drink that while it's still hot."

"But what should we tell them when they come? Actually, we have no idea. After all, it was Lillian and Josh who found that thing," commented Ricki and started to cough.

"I know, but they want to know everything, including when you first saw the bottle in the lake. Just answer their questions, and it'll probably all be over fairly soon."

After Marcus left her room, Ricki ran the events of the fateful evening through her mind once more.

*

Kevin and Cathy had brought the horses home while Ricki's father had driven Lillian, Josh, and Ricki to the hospital to be examined, just to be on the safe side. The police car passed them on the way, with the investigation team who wanted to view the boat and the area around Echo Lake that night.

On the way back from the hospital, Marcus had stopped at the police station and turned in the box with the money.

The officers were amazed to see so much cash.

It was much later that Ricki and her friends found out there was also a key in the box, which police traced to a locker at the train station. There the police found more cash, which probably came from the burglaries as well. It looked like the thief had stored his loot in several different places. Apparently it never occurred to him that his best hiding place, the lockbox in Echo Lake, would be found.

*

"It looks like we exposed a major crime wave," commented Kevin after the police officers left.

"Hmm," was all Ricki said. All of this was no longer important to her. She was much more concerned about the essay on Charlemagne that she'd been assigned, which she would now have to write by herself, since Lillian was probably not well enough to look for her old paper in the boxes in her attic.

"I'll help you, of course," said Kevin. "But I'm wondering if we shouldn't just tell Raymond what happened over the weekend. Maybe he'll give you an extension, or maybe your mother could write you an excuse –"

Ricki laughed bitterly. "Neither one would work. Raymond doesn't care why I'm sick, and if Mom finds out that this is an extra homework assignment that I have to write, she'll really freak out. Oh, no! I'd rather just get down to it and write the thing. The worst that can happen is that I'll have to do another one, but what's one more!"

*

As Lillian left the hospital, leaning on the arms of her parents who had come to pick her up, Dr. Kennedy, accompanied by another doctor, was coming toward her.

"Well, I see you're going home already," said the doctor pleasantly. Lillian nodded.

"Yes, thank goodness. Oh, please, doctor, could you say hello to Lissy Benson for me, and tell her that I'm going to visit her as soon as I feel better? I've known her for a long time, and I just found out that she's in this hospital. Unfortunately, I don't feel well enough to go over to her room just now –"

"Of course! Lissy will be pleased," replied the doctor. He shook Lillian's hand and then walked up the steps to the hospital's entrance with Dr. Albright, while Lillian told her parents about Lissy's riding accident.

*

It was Monday morning, and Ricki's next period was history with Mr. Raymond. The bell had rung a long time ago, but the usually very punctual teacher was nowhere to be seen.

"Maybe he partied all weekend and he's just waking up," joked one of her classmates rudely, and drew laughter from nearly everyone in the class. None of the students in Ricki's class liked the history teacher. He always had something to complain about with all of them. Raymond was just one of those people for whom nothing was ever good enough.

"It looks as though you wrote your paper for nothing," said Kevin, who was sitting on his seat and using his feet to rock back and forth.

"I'd be more than willing to write another one if the next class with that tyrant is canceled!" announced Ricki, looking over Cathy's shoulder. "What are you doing, Cathy?" Ricki asked full of curiosity, and she stretched her neck so that she could see better.

"Reading."

"I can see that, but what?"

"A newspaper article about a certain Carlotta Mancini, who is opening a stable and pastures for old and unwanted horses in our area."

"What? There's a write-up about Carlotta? And you didn't tell us? Hey, read it out loud!" Ricki poked Kevin in the ribs and together they leaned in and listened closely as Cathy read the article to them.

When she had finished, Ricki leaned back. "Well, if that's not good publicity for her ranch, I don't know what is. The journalist really played on the readers' sympathies, and I'll bet the article will make a difference."

Kevin and Cathy nodded in agreement.

"After this article, there are sure to be people who want to support the project. I mean financially."

"Could be. I think Carlotta could use all the financial help she can get. I imagine that a ranch like that will cost a lot of money to run!"

Suddenly, the door opened, and a very pale history teacher entered the room.

"He looks like ten miles of bad road!" someone said, and a lot of kids laughed.

Raymond seemed not to have heard anything. Without reacting to the impolite remark, he walked to his desk and put down his briefcase.

"It's probably best to get this over with," whispered Ricki to her boyfriend as she picked up her paper and went toward the teacher. "Good morning, Mr. Raymond. Here's my essay on Charlemagne," she said. "I hope that it – Mr. Raymond? ... Mr. Raymond! ... Is anything wrong? ... Are you feeling OK?" Ricki stared at her teacher uneasily.

Raymond just waved her aside. "Sit down, Ricki, I'll read the paper another time." His voice sounded flat and raspy.

"There's definitely something wrong with him," Ricki whispered to Cathy on her way back to her seat.

"That's nothing new," Cathy replied, grinning.

What happened next resulted in the strangest history class the students had ever experienced.

Raymond wrote a few dates on the board and asked the students to tell him which wars had happened at those times. Almost all of the answers were wrong, but the teacher just nodded each time, and said, "Right ... good ... OK ..."

"Hey, something weird is going on with him," murmured Kevin. "He's not even listening. Normally, he'd give each one of us an F!"

Ricki shook her head incredulously and looked closely at the teacher. She didn't like him, but she sensed that he was very depressed.

I wonder if he's got family problems? Ricki asked herself. There was a rumor going around school that Raymond and his divorced wife were constantly fighting over their daughter.

Well, thought Ricki, *things can't be too bad. Last week he was his usual mean-spirited, unfair, always-critical self.*

There was a common sigh of relief among the kids when the class, during which Raymond hadn't snapped at anyone, was finally over and the teacher had left the room.

"If this continues, maybe I won't get a D on my report card," grinned Gordon, a tall, skinny kid who seemed to just make it through to the end of each school year by a hair.

*

In chemistry class, which followed history, Mr. Fischer, the teacher, was fiddling with some experiment or other when suddenly there was a loud bang, and the whole room filled with a dense cloud of smoke. The students, coughing and with watering eyes, ran to the open windows in order to get a breath of clean air.

"Someday he's going to blow us all up," groaned Kevin. He tried to fight his increasing nausea with deep breaths of fresh air, and stood watching the street in front of the school. Suddenly he stared, forgetting his nausea for a moment.

"I can't believe it," he said quietly, his eyes growing wide.

"What's up?" Ricki asked, curious to find out what Kevin found so interesting.

"I think I just saw the car!"

"Well, these days there are quite a few!" Ricki replied.

"I mean the one that almost ran Sharazan and me down Friday night!"

Now Kevin had Ricki's full attention. "Are you sure? Did you recognize the license plate number?" she asked excitedly.

Kevin shook his head. "No, it was going too fast this time, but I'm absolutely sure –"

"No kidding?" Ricki stared out of the window, too, but the car had already disappeared.

"Hmmm ... it was the same engine noise, with that awful rattling, not to mention that terrible red paint job. Ricki, I swear, that was it!"

Mr. Fischer clapped his hands, abruptly ending Kevin's speculations. "So, class, that's enough gawking. Let's continue," he said jovially and began to prepare some new experiments. The class groaned in unison.

*

Dr. Albright had finished his examination of Lissy and was now sitting gravely with Dr. Kennedy in Kennedy's office.

"Well, Tom? What do you think?" Kennedy asked, looking his friend directly in the eye. Albright took his time answering. He kept staring at the lists of evaluations, and also at Lissy's X-rays, which were clipped to the illuminated light box on the wall.

"It's definitely a difficult case," he answered finally, tapping his pen on a particular place on one of the X-rays that showed the connection between the neck and the dorsal spinal column.

"Here's the main problem, the one that will be the most difficult! Exactly at this point. Everything else, in comparison, is almost ridiculously easy!"

Dr. Kennedy focused on his friend. He knew, from past experience, that "ridiculously easy" things for Tom Albright always ended up as complicated operations, and when he remembered that, he realized that the "main problem" that he was talking about probably had a zero percent chance of being treated successfully.

"So, you're flying back to Boston tomorrow?" Kennedy asked.

"Have you spoken with the parents?" Tom Albright wanted to know, ignoring his friend's question.

"I did tell them that there was a possibility of bringing in a specialist, but I didn't say anything definite."

"Well, call them in now. Immediately! We need to discuss the situation with them. We need their consent before we can do anything."

"You're really going to operate?"

"Call them before I change my mind. If the parents agree to the operation, we'll begin tomorrow morning at eight o'clock, if that's OK."

Kennedy looked deeply into the eyes of his friend once again. "Are you sure?"

Albright was slowly becoming angry. "Did you bring me all this way so you could argue with me?"

Kennedy reached for the phone and punched in the number for Lissy's father.

"Sometimes I hate being a doctor," he said softly, while Tom watched him pensively.

"Yeah, I know what you mean," he said. "Whatever the outcome – and it can go either way – the responsibility is always ours."

"Did you bring the article with you?" Ricki asked Cathy when she arrived at the stable later that afternoon.

"Of course!" she answered, waving the newspaper. "Carlotta is probably so busy she doesn't have time to read the newspaper right now, so I thought I'd leave it here, and she can take a look at it next time she drops by."

"Let me see it again." Carefully Ricki reread what Cathy had read to them earlier. "That's a really good piece," she said and was just about to hand the paper back to Cathy when she noticed the headline on the last page: "Weeks of Research by the Organization for the Protection of Species Fails Due to Pedestrians' Nighttime Walks."

"Wait, that's interesting," said Ricki and skimmed the article. "They really did observe the wild ducks around Echo Lake day and night, and even took eggs out of the nests so they could hatch them in incubators. It says they set up little cameras to ... well, that doesn't interest me as much. It's enough for me if the little guys are there and don't land in a cooking pot."

"And what was that about the pedestrians?" asked Cathy, looking at Ricki expectantly.

"There were some idiots out walking who disturbed the animals at night, and that caused them to leave their nests in fear, and now the organization is worried about the consequences that will have for that species. Some people! I mean the pedestrians!" added Ricki.

Cathy took back the newspaper and looked at the article Ricki had just mentioned. She turned pale. "You didn't read to the end, did you?" she asked Ricki, who had grabbed

131

a broom and had already started sweeping out the stable corridor.

"Nope," she admitted easily and then hesitated. "Why?"

"I think the idiots were us, Ricki," she said softly and let herself plop onto a bale of hay.

"What? Are you crazy? Why would we –?"

"Farther down, they write something about horseback riders, and it was Friday night that the men from the organization were there to get the research results."

Pale and remorseful, the two girls looked at each other.

"We may have ruined everything for them. I'm feeling really guilty!"

"Me, too, but on the other hand we gave the police some evidence that will help them solve the burglary cases," Ricki said, trying to justify their actions.

"True ... but the ducks are gone!"

Silently Ricki sat down next to Cathy, and the two girls struggled with their guilty consciences.

"Do you think we should call the organization and tell them that we were the idiots?" asked Ricki.

"I think they'll find out by themselves. When the police clear up the burglaries, they'll report it in the newspaper, and then it will come out that we were on Echo Lake Friday night."

"What a mess!"

"Hello, is anyone home?" Josh called into the stable from the courtyard, his voice sounding as happy as always.

"Hey, Josh, how's it going? Are you on your way to see Lillian?" Ricki had gotten up and gone outside to greet him. "Hello, Cherish, how are you?"

"My little piebald mare is always fine! How's Diablo? Is he OK?"

Ricki nodded. "And Lillian?"

"She's much better. She doesn't have a headache anymore, and she expects to be fine in a few days. But it'll be a while before she can go riding again. The elbow still looks pretty bad and gives her pain. But she really wants to visit that girl in the hospital ... what's her name? Lissy, right?"

Ricki nodded again.

"Say, you really look upset today. Did something happen?" Josh looked closely at Ricki.

"You could say that, couldn't you, Cathy?" She looked for help to her girlfriend, who had come outside, too.

"Have you read the paper today?" she asked Josh, who was grinning broadly.

"Do you mean the terrific article about Carlotta's future ranch, or the somewhat less flattering lines about us?"

Bewildered, Ricki and Cathy looked at Lillian's boyfriend.

"You know about it and can still laugh about it?" Ricki asked, amazed.

"Well, if I cry it won't bring the wild ducks back, will it?" Josh could tell how bad the girls felt.

"Don't worry about it too much," he tried to console them. "Researchers experience failures every once in a while, and what happened Friday evening probably isn't the first or won't be the last time in the history of the organization. Anyway, I've already talked with Richie and Jack, who carried out these nightly expeditions, and told them about what happened that night on Echo Lake." He laughed.

"They now have a tremendous respect for you and Diablo,"

he said to Ricki. "Plus, Richie said that the head of the Organization for Species Protection, Professor Langdon, has more research planned for next year, and then they intend to fence in a large area so that the experiment doesn't fail again."

"And ... and they're not mad at us?" Ricki asked cautiously.

"Well, no. But Jack's just upset about all of his sleepless nights."

When Josh saw Ricki's doubtful face, he added quickly, "Those two guys can't be angry! They're really great, and right now they're totally exhausted. By the way, they're members of our Western Club. Oh, I almost forgot. They dropped by a few days ago, at my suggestion, to find out when the best time would be to meet with Carlotta, but you weren't home. It's about an old horse whose owner died recently. They're looking for a stall for him. I thought that when Carlotta's ranch is finished there would probably be an opening for him."

Ricki and Cathy looked knowingly at each other.

"Then it was Richie and Jack who were hanging around here, and at Lillian's? And we thought they were the burglars!"

Relieved, the girls laughed.

"I have to go now," said Josh. "Say hello to Kevin for me when you see him."

"Sure thing. Hey, that's a great saddle," Ricki noticed at the last minute, before the young man urged Cherish to get going.

"Yeah. But I'm only allowed to borrow it until mine is dry and the girth is mended." He grinned. "Which is too bad. I could really get used to this one."

Chapter 9

Lissy's father sat collapsed in one of the deep armchairs in the waiting area for the operating room, wringing his hands continuously. The tension was visible on his pale face and he seemed to have aged considerably in the last seven and a half hours that he'd spent at the hospital. From time to time he glanced at the blond hollow-cheeked woman who paced back and forth in front of the window.

"Can't you sit down? Your pacing is driving me crazy!" he said, breaking the silence and staring at her intensely.

"Leave me alone!" Virginia Benson's nerves were as raw as Edmund's. "How could you have given your permission for this operation?" she shouted at him. "What if the child can't move at all, or if she ... if she should ... die?" Virginia hid her face in her hands and began to sob.

"You know that ... that this operation is her only hope to get well again," Edmund answered, his voice trembling and his whole being both physically and emotionally exhausted. "And anyway, it was Lissy's own decision to have the operation, after the doctor –"

"Never!" the woman kept screaming. "I would never

have allowed this ... this death sentence! Why didn't you let me know earlier?"

"I tried to, but you, as is so often the case, weren't available!" Edmund felt an uncontrollable rage growing inside. "Anyway, what do you mean, 'death sentence'? Don't say things like that! It makes me crazy!"

"You *are* crazy!"

"Virginia, that's enough!" Edmund's voice became dangerously quiet.

Lissy's mother sobbed quietly to herself. The fear she felt for her daughter seemed to be more than she could endure.

Edmund stared through the glass pane in the waiting room door at the little light above the door to the operating room. It would remain on until Lissy's operation was finished.

How much longer? he thought, tortured, and closed his weary eyes. *How can it be that Lissy's operation can take so long? Or is she perhaps – No! No! No! God, please, let her be OK, and let that light go out.*

*

"Hey, have you heard the latest?" Josh had just begun calling around to his friends. Now he had Ricki on the phone.

"No, tell me!"

"There were two policemen at my house a few minutes ago!"

"Why? Because of the ducks?" Ricki asked in a panicky voice.

"Ducks? No, they said that we're going to get a reward for finding the money! Are you sitting down? For our help in

136

retrieving the money stolen in the burglaries we're getting a reward of two thousand dollars! Can you believe it, Ricki?"

"No way!" Now Ricki had to sit down.

"It's true! What do you think? Wasn't the nighttime swim worth it?" joked Josh.

"I'm not sure," the girl answered slowly. "I risked the life of my horse, irresponsibly, and all the money in the world can't change that!"

"Now listen, Ricki Sulai!" The young man had become deadly serious. "You acted on impulse to help us, and the only possibility that you saw was to use Diablo. Believe me, Ricki, a horse has much better instincts than a human. And you can be sure that if Diablo had felt himself – or you – to be in danger he wouldn't even have gone into the water. Do you understand?"

"Are you sure?" responded Ricki, wanting to believe Josh.

"Yes!"

For a moment, no one spoke.

"Can't you see the good side? You and Diablo brought us back to shore safely so that Lillian could be cared for. You and your horse performed beautifully. Stop blaming yourself. Just be proud of your horse! You don't find an animal that brave every day."

Ricki sniffed. "He really is the best thing that's ever happened to me," she said softly.

"Finally, you understand. And now just be happy that everything ended so well, and stop tormenting yourself imagining all the things that could have gone wrong, OK?"

"OK!"

"Promise?"

Ricki took a deep breath. "Promise. But now you'll have

137

to excuse me. I told Jake I would help him clean out the stall of my fabulous horse!"

"Good! That's the spirit. Go look after Diablo. I'm going to call the others and then I'm coming over to the stable, too. Take care, Ricki. See you later."

*

Edmund sat on his daughter's bed. She was in her plaster cast and her head was once again held in position by a monstrous metal frame.

Very carefully, he held Lissy's small hand in his, and kept stroking it, while Virginia stood at the foot of the bed, a moist handkerchief pressed against her nose.

"We've done everything in our power," Dr. Albright had said an hour before, when Lissy, pale and still unconscious from the anesthesia, was moved out of the operating room into the recovery room. "It is entirely possible that your daughter will be able to move again normally. But don't expect this to happen overnight. We'll have to be very, very patient and let time work for us. Do you understand?"

Edmund nodded. It was impossible for him to say anything at that moment. Gratefully, he grabbed the surgeon's hand as tears of joy ran down his cheeks.

Virginia stared at the completely motionless face of her child as her gurney was pushed past her. She was convinced that the doctor, who was standing there in front of her, had just told her the biggest lie of his life. She just couldn't believe that one day her daughter would be OK.

The way Lissy looks now, I can't imagine she'll ever be well again, she thought.

"It's all your fault," Virginia raged at Edmund again. "I never wanted her to have a horse, let alone jump in horse shows! But you ... you fulfilled her every wish. You always gave her whatever she wanted, just to take her away from me! That's the only reason you gave her that horrid animal. *You* made her into ... a cripple!"

Then, without warning, she turned on Edmund and began to beat him on the back with her fists. "I hate you! I hate you! I hate you!" she screamed, until she was so exhausted all she could was sob.

Dr. Kennedy, still in his surgical scrubs, put his arms around Lissy's mother and drew her gently away from Edmund, who just looked at her sadly.

"You'll feel differently soon ... the whole world will look different to you ... and, Mrs. Benson, it's time for you to begin thinking about where you would like to go on your first walk with your daughter."

"Does that mean ... she ... she really will be ... completely cured?" stammered Virginia, tonelessly and stared at Dr. Kennedy with enormous eyes.

He nodded and looked over at Dr. Albright, who was talking quietly to Edmund.

"That man over there," he said, "is a great doctor, a gifted surgeon. He has so much more talent than the rest of us. I'm proud to call him my friend."

*

The next day, Ricki, Cathy, and Kevin visited Lillian.

"I've really missed you guys," the girl beamed, as the three trooped into her room.

"Lily, we're so glad you're feeling better!" Ricki wrapped her arms around her friend's neck and she sat down on the edge of the bed.

"Well, I'm not quite over it yet! I'm still a little dizzy when I stand up, but that'll go away."

She reached for Ricki's hand. "Did I ever thank you?" she asked, but Ricki just waved her off.

"Forget it! If you want to thank someone, thank Diablo. After all, he's the one who pulled you out of the water."

"Hey, Ricki, move over!" Kevin pulled her to the side so that Cathy could give Lillian the big bouquet of flowers she'd brought.

"Best wishes from all of us for a speedy recovery," she exclaimed as she handed the flowers to her friend.

"Oh, they're beautiful. You guys are too much! I should really –"

"Lillian, be quiet!" grinned Kevin.

"OK!" Lillian clammed up immediately, but she couldn't stay quiet for long. "Hey, what are you planning on doing today? Are you going riding?"

"I think so, maybe later," replied Ricki.

"Did Josh tell you about the reward?" Kevin wanted to know.

"Of course! Great, isn't it?" Lillian's eyes sparkled. "Hey, what should we do with all that money?"

"I don't know, but I'm sure we'll think of something."

"Do they know who stole the money?" asked Cathy.

"I don't think so! Josh told me they're searching for a car that was parked near several of the houses that were broken into," Lillian told them.

"A car?" Kevin was all ears. "That wouldn't be the same

car that –" He looked over at Ricki, who knew exactly what he was going to say.

"Maybe. Do you still remember the license number?"

"Of course, at least part of it."

"I think you should tell that to the police." Ricki said to her boyfriend.

"Yeah, I think I will."

"Could you do me a favor?" Lillian asked.

"Sure! Whatever you want! How'd you like us to bring Holli to your room?"

Lillian sighed. "Ah, that'd be great, but I don't think my mother would like it very much, especially since the vacuum cleaner won't suck up horse manure," the girl grinned. "No, something completely different. Actually, I wanted to visit Lissy Benson in the hospital today, but unfortunately I'm still in bed, as you can see. I was just thinking, if you don't have anything else planned, you could go in my place. I'm sure she'd love the company."

"But we don't even know her," objected Cathy. Lillian just made a dismissive gesture.

"That's not important. Lissy is really nice. You don't have to become best friends, just give her my best wishes and say hi from me. I don't want her to think I've forgotten her!"

"Sure. Why shouldn't we go?" Ricki asked. "I think if you're in the hospital, you'd be glad to have any visitors!"

Kevin was a little reserved. "I'm not sure I can do it," he admitted freely. "I'd probably stare at her legs the whole time. Not on purpose, of course, but when I think about your friend being paralyzed forever, it upsets me so much that it almost makes me sick to my stomach."

"At least you're honest, Kevin." Ricki said, and squeezed her boyfriend's hand. "But we are going to visit her, and you're going to give her one of your charming smiles so she realizes that she is an attractive person in spite of her condition, and that we are glad to visit her even though she can't move."

"OK!" Kevin gave in. "When do you want to go?"

"Go right now. I think she needs visitors much more than I do," urged Lillian. Then she held the bouquet of flowers up in the air.

"Please, don't think me ungrateful, but it would be nice if you took these wonderful flowers to Lissy. They'll brighten up her hospital room."

"Well, then, I think we should hurry before the flowers start to wilt," Ricki laughed and kissed Lillian on the cheek. "Get well. I want to have you with us when we go riding this weekend."

"OK, Ricki. I'll do my best. Now get outta here! A little sleep will do me some good."

"See you, Lily."

"Take care!"

"We'll be back soon!"

Lillian waved good-bye to her friends, and then she closed her eyes. *Lissy will be pleased*, she thought as she drifted off to sleep.

*

Ricki, Kevin, and Cathy rode their bikes to the hospital parking lot, taking several shortcuts along the way.

"When I think about this visit, it makes me really un-

142

easy," groaned Kevin for the third time. Ricki, growing tired of his whining, made a face.

"Oh, come on, I'm sure that there are worse things!" she said as she maneuvered her bike into a space in the bike rack, which was near the huge arched entrance to the hospital.

"But I hate hospitals!" The boy tried one last time to get out of having to see Lissy. He was starting to turn green.

"Kevin, enough! Your continuous whining is getting on my nerves." Ricki looked at her boyfriend earnestly. "We're all horseback riders, as is Lissy," she reminded him. "And this terrible accident could have happened to any one of us. How would you feel if you were in her place and nobody wanted to visit you because you couldn't walk anymore? Would you think that was OK? Or what if I were lying there –?"

Kevin lowered his head in shame. "You're right, Ricki. It's just that I feel so helpless, guilty even, because I'm healthy, and she's –"

"You ... sweetheart!" Lovingly she pushed him toward the entrance. "Healthy people can help sick people get better, isn't that true? So let's go, OK?"

The boy nodded. Once again, as he had at the lake, he realized that he could learn something from Ricki and her approach toward all kinds of problems. In many ways, he admired her greatly.

As he walked to the steps of the hospital, he dropped the key to his bicycle lock. He turned around and bent down to retrieve it. When he got up, he started and then stared at the parking lot in front of him.

"Are you coming?" He heard Ricki's impatient voice, but he didn't respond to it.

Mesmerized, he stood gaping at a dirty red car, which was parked a little haphazardly. Slowly Kevin walked around another car and almost twisted his neck trying to see the license plate.

Kevin held his breath. Was this the car they were looking for?

"It's here!" The boy turned toward Ricki, who was getting irritated with her boyfriend.

"What?"

"The car!"

Ricki and Cathy hurried over to Kevin.

"If you're sure, call the police!" said Cathy.

"And if I'm wrong?" asked Ricki's boyfriend uneasily.

"At least your conscience will be clear."

"Hmm. OK! Will you guys wait here?"

"No, we're coming with you, and as soon as you've called them, we're going to visit Lissy!" decided Ricki, and together they took the steps three at a time and went through the glass doors into the hospital lobby. There was a phone booth just inside the entrance, and Kevin called the police station while Ricki and Cathy waited nervously.

"OK," said Kevin, a few seconds later. "They're coming to take a look. "I told them that we'll be in Lissy Benson's room, in case they have any more questions."

"Good, but let's get going. We don't want to miss visiting hours."

*

"I have a problem, Doctor," stammered Edmund, embarrassed, as he stood in front of the two doctors in Kennedy's

144

office. "Your fee for the operation ... I don't know how I'm going to manage it."

"Well," Dr. Albright smiled, "we can't undo the operation just because you can't pay for it. The important thing is that the procedure was successful. We'll figure out the rest somehow."

Edmund shook his head. "It's really upsetting me, especially since my salary isn't very large and I have to pay alimony to my ex-wife, and child support for my daughter and her little brother."

"We'll think of something," replied Dr. Kennedy as he gently ushered Edmund out of the room. "Go back to your daughter. Everything else will take care of itself."

Let's hope so, thought Edmund, disheartened, as he walked slowly along the hospital corridor. *It could all have been so easy if only –*

As he approached Lissy's room, he heard several voices talking and laughing together.

"You met Lillian as she was lying on her stomach in the mud in the middle of the riding ring?" giggled Ricki, as Edmund reached the door.

"Yeah, she looked like a mud pie, and Doc Holliday stood next to her, completely oblivious!" Lissy's voice still sounded a little weak, but her father could finally hear a little life in her.

"You said you were at the Summersfield Ranch. Did you know our friend Jake Alcott back then? He used to work there," asked Kevin, relieved to see that he wasn't as uncomfortable with Lissy's condition as he thought he'd be.

"Yeah. He's a really nice guy! I was so happy to see him when he dropped by the other day," said Lissy, and her eyes began to glisten. "I didn't know then that I was going to be operated on, and that I was going to be OK."

"What? You ... you're not ... you're ... I mean, you're not going to stay ... paralyzed?" Kevin stuttered.

"Kevin, you are really impossible!" Ricki exclaimed and looked at her boyfriend in exasperation.

"Oh, leave him alone, it's OK!" smiled Lissy. "Yes, I'll walk again some day and be able to move almost normally, but it's going to take a long time."

"That doesn't matter!" Ricki and her friends were really happy for the young woman. "Lillian and Jake will be ecstatic when we tell them the good news!"

Edmund's face turned grim. *Those voices. Don't those voices belong to those kids, who –?*

He opened the door, his heart beating wildly, and stepped in unnoticed by the kids, who were standing with their backs to him. Only Lissy could see him. Her face lit up.

"Dad! I want to introduce you to Ricki, Cathy, and Kevin! They're friends of Lillian Bates, whom I met at a riding workshop at Summersfield. Look at the beautiful bouquet of flowers they brought me. Dad, is something wrong? You look so weird –"

"Ricki Sulai, Kevin Thomas, and Cathy Sutherland," said Edmund slowly, as the three friends jumped at the sound of the voice they knew so well.

"You know each other? That's wild!" Lissy was astonished. "Well, I should have known. After all, Dad is a teacher ..."

"Mr. Raymond?" Ricki actually held her breath. She never expected that her history teacher would turn up here.

"That's your father? Are you sure? I mean ... I thought

146

your name is Benson," Kevin, confused, stumbled over the words.

Lissy had to laugh at that. "I'm sure, Kevin. My parents are divorced, and I have my mother's maiden name. And he –" she looked at her father lovingly, "he's the best dad in the world," she said quietly.

Edmund Raymond was visibly touched, but Ricki and her friends were flabbergasted.

That mean, unfair, impatient, bad-tempered teacher is supposed to be the best dad in the world? Before I believe that, I'd believe that Diablo will turn white by tomorrow, thought Ricki, but she didn't let her thoughts show.

"I think we'd better go now, Lissy. But we'll definitely come back," Ricki said, avoiding Raymond's stare.

"But soon, OK? And tell Lillian that I can't wait to see her. And say hello to Jake for me, and tell him how much I appreciated his dropping by to see me, OK?" Lissy's eyes told the story. She had the feeling that she'd just made three new wonderful friends.

As they tried to get past Raymond, the door opened again, and two policemen came in.

"Mr. Edmund Raymond?" one of them asked.

Edmund turned pale and nodded, his eyes downcast.

Lissy looked bewildered. "Dad? What are they doing here?"

"May we speak with you for a moment?" asked the officer, with a sidelong glance at Lissy.

Raymond nodded weakly and glanced one more time at his beloved daughter. "Don't worry, honey. They just want me to answer a few questions." Tenderly he blew her a few kisses and then he left the room, his head held high. He knew that the policemen would arrest him, and he was grateful to them that they hadn't done it in the presence of his daughter. He would have the opportunity of telling her everything later, and he was sure that she would understand.

Outside, in the corridor, Ricki, Cathy, and Kevin overheard the policemen arrest their teacher and advise him of his rights. They turned pale. *Raymond had committed the burglaries? But why?*

"I'm glad it's finally over," Raymond said softly to the policemen. He glanced at the closed hospital room door, behind which his daughter lay. "How did you figure out that it was me?"

"Based on your license plate number and several witnesses, we were able to identify your car."

Raymond nodded slightly and looked over at the kids knowingly.

Kevin had the feeling that his legs would give way any minute. "Mr. Raymond, I ... I'm sorry," he stammered, but the teacher just put his hand gently on the boy's shoulder.

"It's OK, Kevin. I've been carrying this burden around with me for weeks now, and I'm just glad that it's over. I was going to turn myself in some time in the next few weeks anyway, when Lissy was a little better. I did it for her. How else could I have paid for the operation? But it didn't turn out as I'd imagined, and –" He tried to smile through his tears. "What irony. Doctor Albright operated on Lissy without any guarantee of payment. If I'd known that, none of this would have happened."

Suddenly Ricki understood why Lissy loved her father so much. *He went so far as to steal just so he could pay for his*

148

daughter's operation, she thought, deeply moved, and now she felt sorry for the teacher.

"Mr. Raymond, I have some more good news for you!" Dr. Kennedy hurried along the corridor, and stopped suddenly right in front of Lissy's father when he saw the two policemen and the three friends.

"May I ask what you're all doing here?" he asked gravely. "And may I remind you that the young woman behind this door has just undergone a very serious operation and should not be disturbed or upset?" Angrily, Dr, Kennedy stared at the policemen and the three friends.

"Please, all of you, leave, except for immediate family!" The tone of his voice told them all that there would be no arguing this point.

Ricki, Cathy, and Kevin rushed past him and ran down the hallway, while the two policemen just looked at each other undecided.

"You, too!" said Kennedy to the police, but one of them pointed at Raymond.

"I'm sorry, Doctor, but we have to take him with us. He has confessed to the recent burglaries in town."

"Is there any chance you're mistaken?" he asked the officers, looking at Raymond.

"None."

Dr. Kennedy pressed his lips together, and then looked at the teacher, who had almost collapsed, and shook his head.

"Please, Doctor, what's the good news?" he asked.

"We ... I had a long talk with your insurance company, Mr. Raymond, and with the assistance of Doctor Albright's explanations they've changed their minds and agreed to cover all the costs of Lissy's operation!"

Raymond smiled. "That's wonderful! Thank you from the bottom of my heart, Doctor. Please, take good care of my child." Turning to the police officers, he asked, "Shall we go?" They nodded silently and led him out of the hospital.

*

Lillian and Jake were elated when Ricki told them about Lissy's successful operation. But they were both shocked and saddened to hear about Raymond's crime spree. However, since they knew why the teacher had done it, they didn't judge him harshly. He hadn't wanted to enrich himself with the money; he had just wanted to pay for his beloved daughter's operation.

*

The judge at Raymond's trial reasoned similarly. Ricki and her friends, including Josh, had been subpoenaed to appear as witnesses, as was Dr. Kennedy. In addition, the people from whom Raymond had stolen were asked to testify, but even they seemed to have some compassion for the teacher because of Lissy's condition and because all of the money had been found and returned. Raymond repeated over and over how much he regretted the whole thing and, with drooping shoulders, he apologized to each one of them formally.

At the end of the trial, he was able to smile gratefully, because he was given a probationary sentence.

"I am so happy," he said later to Ricki, Cathy, and Kevin, who had waited for him on the street after the trial.

"Lissy will be so relieved," said Ricki with a smile and she shook her teacher's hand.

Raymond nodded. "Ricki, can you forgive me for Joan of Arc and Charlemagne?" he asked the girl.

"That crime comes under the terms of the probation as well," grinned Ricki, before she and her friends walked over to join Josh and Lillian, who were standing a discreet distance away.

"I really have misjudged those kids," whispered Raymond to himself as he watched them go.

*

It was the first time since their moonlight adventure that the friends set out together for a long ride on their horses.

"I can tell you guys one thing," said Ricki as she tightened Diablo's saddle girth. "I don't want to see Echo Lake even from a distance today!"

"No problem," replied Kevin and led Sharazan out of the stable in front of Diablo into the yard, where the others were waiting with their horses already saddled.

"Hey, have you guys decided yet what we should do with the reward money?" asked Josh.

"I have an idea!" Ricki shortened the reins and mounted.

"Well, tell us!"

"I'd like to give Carlotta the money for Mercy Ranch, so that she can use it for the horses in the future!"

For a moment there was silence among the young people, and then Lillian burst out: "Well, that's the best idea you've had in a while. You have my vote!"

"Mine, too, of course!"

"Brilliant!"

Ricki grinned.

"Well, if that's the way it is, I suggest we ride over to Carlotta's right now and bring her the good news personally," she said, and stroked Diablo's shiny neck.

"That, Ricki Sulai, is the second best idea of the day!" exclaimed Josh, before they all rode away in high spirits.

Twenty minutes later they could be seen galloping across a wide meadow. They couldn't wait to see the look of surprise on Carlotta's face.